...E...SHIRE COUNTY COUNCIL
ED........D C..........CES.

D0418868

SPECIAL MESSAGE TO READERS

This book is published under the auspices of

THE ULVERSCROFT FOUNDATION

(registered charity No. 264873 UK)

Established in 1972 to provide funds for research, diagnosis and treatment of eye diseases. Examples of contributions made are: —

A Children's Assessment Unit at Moorfield's Hospital, London.

•

Twin operating theatres at the Western Ophthalmic Hospital, London.

•

A Chair of Ophthalmology at the Royal Australian College of Ophthalmologists.

•

The Ulverscroft Children's Eye Unit at the Great Ormond Street Hospital For Sick Children, London.

You can help further the work of the Foundation by making a donation or leaving a legacy. Every contribution, no matter how small, is received with gratitude. Please write for details to:

**THE ULVERSCROFT FOUNDATION,
The Green, Bradgate Road, Anstey,
Leicester LE7 7FU, England.
Telephone: (0116) 236 4325**

**In Australia write to:
THE ULVERSCROFT FOUNDATION,
c/o The Royal Australian and New Zealand
College of Ophthalmologists,
94-98 Chalmers Street, Surry Hills,
N.S.W. 2010, Australia**

Sally Rena was born in Scotland and lived there until the age of sixteen. She is convent educated and spent two years of further education in France and Italy. In 1964 she won the Vogue Talent Contest and now lives in London with her husband and four children.

THE SEA ROAD WEST

The road from the Scottish mainland to
Kintillo lay across a ridge of forbidding
hills, a natural barrier isolating the
peninsula and making Kintillo a place of
both refuge and loneliness. The trouble
began with the dying of Father Macabe
and the arrival of the young and idealistic
Father James. The unusually hot weather
that summer, the isolation and odd
coincidences combined to produce a
tragedy which remained in the villagers'
memory for many years. Passions hidden
below the surface erupted in a violent
upsurge of love, hatred and jealousy which
swept Kintillo like a storm.

SALLY RENA

THE
SEA ROAD
WEST

Complete and Unabridged

ULVERSCROFT
Leicester

First published in Great Britain in 1975

First Large Print Edition
published 2003

Copyright © 1975 by Sally Rena
All rights reserved

British Library CIP Data

Rena, Sally, *1941* –
    The sea road west.—Large print ed.—
    Ulverscroft large print series: general fiction
    1. Large type books
    I. Title
    823.9'14 [F]

    ISBN 1–8439–5101–0

LINCOLNSHIRE
COUNTY COUNCIL

Published by
F. A. Thorpe (Publishing)
Anstey, Leicestershire

Set by Words & Graphics Ltd.
Anstey, Leicestershire
Printed and bound in Great Britain by
T. J. International Ltd., Padstow, Cornwall

This book is printed on acid-free paper

To my husband, my sons
and daughters

1

Kintillo is cut off from Wester Ross by high ridges of sandstone that rise up like a wall against the mainland and slope down on the southern side into the sea. One road goes over the summit of these hills and so long as the snow lasts Kintillo is an island. When the spring comes the pass is cut up with streams and the mists settle down on the heights for days at a time. Even in the summer there are scarcely three days together when the sky is clear, when the puddles dry up in the ruts of the road and when the mountain streams are quiet.

When the weather is warm enough the women of Kintillo village take out their kitchen chairs and sit by the sea wall. And they carry their knitting with them and cups of tea, so that even though they are sitting in the sun their hands and mouths are busy. Depending on the angle of the kitchen chairs, there is a view of the whole bay, the lodge gates to Kintillo House and the rectory on its hump of hill beyond, and no one can drive down the road from the pass without being noticed and discussed.

When the women go back across the road to cook the midday meal or when they leave their chairs to go shouting over the wall where the children are playing on the beach, the chairs are left in a semicircle like a court-room adjourned. And this clique of women is a constant reminder of a certain scandal, five years ago, in which one man lost his mind and another died.

From the beginning of July, that summer, until the end of August, the weather was unusually hot and almost no rain fell during those two months. The crops of barley and spring wheat grew on thin soil in the valley, and without water they sprang up in thin irregular tufts and the grain in the husks was as small and hard as stones. The drainage ditches on the moors dried up, and the sheep came down to the peat loch Doonican where many of them drowned in the mud on the stagnant shores. In this abnormal heat there was too much quarrelling in the airless evenings and several unwanted babies were conceived among the three villages of the peninsula.

The weather was blamed for everything, and most of all for the tragedy which followed. But the truth was simply a set of coincidences, like seeds blown in on the wind that landed on the same patch of ground and became entangled when they started to grow.

★　★　★

The trouble that year began with the dying of Father Macabe, the Catholic priest. Father Macabe was a dull man. When he preached the Sunday sermon the babies in the congregation began to cry. The small children sucked the tops of the church pews and crawled about under the seats. And a restless tension set in among the adults, who yawned and swatted at the children with their prayer books. When Father Macabe paid a call on his parishioners, most of them remembered, the minute he was in the door, several things that urgently had to be done; and while he was there they would be getting up and down in their chairs, practically dusting under his feet or doing the weekly accounts in front of him. And even those people who had plenty to complain about became dissatisfied after half an hour of uninterrupted moaning because he was certain to agree with everything they said and he would stare at them with his wet brown eyes until the last of the home-made scones was eaten and the teapot was empty. For eight years Father Macabe served the parishes of Kintillo and

Stromeferry with as much effect as a stone embedded in a stream — he was worn away by his work and no one noticed until the day he left for a week's holiday and did not come back.

The next Sunday Father Lanni drove across the pass from Dornie, forty miles to the south, to say mass and hear confessions. After the mass was ended he leaned one hand against the edge of the pulpit and fiddled with the notes on the lectern. He cleared his throat and stared out across the heads of the congregation. 'Dearly beloved brethren,' he said, 'your prayers are asked for your parish priest Father Macabe, at present gravely ill.'

Directly the church doors had opened, Father Lanni drove off in a great hurry back to Dornie as though the cares of these two parishes pursued him. But Father Macabe became a hero. In the following weeks the details of his illness were put together in whispers and sentences half finished and only one thing was certain among the tangle of rumours — Father Macabe was dying and would not come back to Kintillo. The tumour in his stomach had been removed but others grew up like knots in a heavy chain that stretched from his lungs to his intestines. Though these details were often discussed, the word cancer was never mentioned; it was like a spell cast on the minds of children.

But Father Macabe came back, one hot close day at the end of June when the sea lay as heavy as oil in the bay and the birds were quiet on the shore. As the taxi passed by up the beach road, there were the usual numbers of women and children staring out from the cottage doors and the same number of dogs chased the car across the bay. The dogs were luckier than the women and children for they must have seen the dying priest clearly in every detail although they came back to lie in the shade as if nothing had happened. For two days no one went near the rectory and Father Macabe was nursed alone by his housekeeper. Father Macabe was neither a landowner nor a peasant — he came from the middle classes of Aberdeen and his only intimate friend was Father Lanni from Dornie. Besides, what can be said to a man who is dying when every word uttered reminds him of the good things in the life he is leaving behind? So out of shyness the village people left him alone, and only from time to time in the course of those three days a few of them looked up at the rectory on its hill across the bay and thought that they understood why he had come back. From the rectory windows the dying priest could see the great peaks of the Cuillins rising from the soft coast hills across the water. When he had pain to fight he could do that without distraction, in the vast silence of an empty land, and when he died, the people of the villages believed that his soul, like theirs, would be carried out to sea on bars of light one after another towards the setting sun.

On the third night after Father Macabe had returned, the brazen Murdo Mackenzie went up the hill to call on him with the small pretext of crab-apple jam as a present. By the time he had been up there an hour, most of the village knew where he was; the pub was full and the crowd which had gathered overflowed into the street and across it by the sea wall. There was nothing whatsoever to do but drink. The air inside the pub was stifling with smoke and stale beer and outside the night was as cold as April without a stir of wind. There were times that summer, when the twilight seemed to linger on too long. Flecks of the night as thick as moths began to gather in the air, the land and the sky began to merge, and still there was enough light to see by. When Murdo Mackenzie came back down the hill he was pale and distorted by the coming night and his body seemed to float above the ground. There was a hush among the people standing round the pub door as they listened to the sound of his footsteps in the shadows of the village street and the atmosphere of the evening, which had been bored and slack, tightened like a trip wire. Murdo seemed to swell with importance as he came into the light and, though the bottom half of his face was solemn and sad, his eyes shone with excitement.

No one spoke. His cousin bought him a drink and small groups of men broke up and came over casually to where he stood. Murdo drank the whole pint of beer and wiped his mouth with the back of his hand. Presently he stared in a sad way at the dregs of his mug and hitched at the string round his trouser tops with his free hand. No one moved.

Finally his cousin said, 'Well how is he then? Since you're waiting to tell us.'

'Terrible,' Murdo said. 'Just terrible.'

He put the beer mug down on the top of the sea wall and steadied it carefully so it should not fall off, and then he began to speak. 'When I came in the room', he said, 'there was just this candle burning by the bed. There was this bitter smell — medicines, injections, jars of all sorts — and Father Macabe was lying quite still there in the bed.' He gazed at the light that hung above the pub door. A few moths flickered about the light and Murdo squinted his eyes and spoke with his voice a little lifted. 'As true as I'm standing here,' he went on, 'he was lying so still I thought the poor man was already gone. His eyes hung loose in the sockets ready to fall out and his hands were spread out stiff on the covers.'

Although it was unfortunate to have to listen to him bragging about the suffering of Father Macabe, nobody moved away. 'I put the pot of jam down on the bedside table,' said Murdo, 'and I went to sit down by the bed where he could see me plainly in the light. At that, he moved a little and he asked me in a whisper to wet his lips for his throat was dry. When I'd done this, he was able to speak quite clearly and asked after my family and the relatives. But he had something on his mind, agitating him, and after a bit he began to describe to me what they did to him in the hospital.'

Murdo still spoke in a grave slow voice but he raised it a little so that those who had just then come out of the pub could hear him clearly. 'They removed,' he said, 'a growth the size and shape of a pineapple from the wall of his stomach. They operated on him maybe three times in the next few weeks and each time there was another one, bigger and more terrible than the rest. By the time they had done with him, most of his insides were gone and his suffering was terrible. Sometimes while he was speaking I had to get up from the chair and wipe the perspiration from his forehead for it was rolling into his eyes. And then towards the end of his stay in hospital, he could keep nothing down and was fainting from the pain. There was nothing left to be done but to ring up his mother in Aberdeen and prepare her for the death . . . '

At the bold use of the word death, several of those who had been listening most closely began to move away and to pay more attention to their drinks. And though Murdo went on elaborating on the sufferings of the priest the thread of attention had snapped. It was cold outside. The night had finally come and with it a mean little wind that blew dust and bits of rubbish along the street and most of Murdo's audience were suddenly anxious to get back inside the pub. From the shadows just inside the pub door a clear sad voice rose up. The lobsterman Danny started singing some nights when it was getting late and he was drunk, the Song of the Summer Isles. He had never been there, but he sang with such infinite longing that for many people who listened the Summer Isles were Paradise, a place they had believed in when they were children and never found in all the years afterwards. But that particular night as the lobsterman went home, balancing gently against the houses and tripping over the doorsteps, he went on singing. His voice trailed out behind him and remained in the minds of the people who followed him, a lament for Father Macabe.

Murdo Mackenzie stood and watched Danny go by, with his arms slack by his sides and a queer look of shame in his face, and once or twice before he left the pub he glanced up to the point where the rectory stood on the hill and looked away again quickly.

The following morning before the village shop was open, Miss Morag, the priest's housekeeper, came running down the beach road as fast as her clumsy legs would take her. Her face in the morning light was a sickly yellow and her story was repeated several times before it made any sense. It seemed that when Murdo Mackenzie had walked up to the rectory the evening before in the twilight, perhaps to do with the staring face of Miss Morag in the doorway, and perhaps to do with the cramped darkness in the rectory hall, he had taken fright. He had thrust the pot of crab-apple jam into her hands and rushed out the back way, stumbling over the coal scuttle in the kitchen and knocking the lid off the dustbin outside. He had sat for an hour on the shoulder of the hill, never moving except to light a cigarette and all this time Miss Morag had watched him until he came back through the shadows of the sycamores and set off down the road to the pub.

As near as she was able to judge in her loose-witted way, it was about the time that Murdo fell over the coal scuttle by the kitchen range that Father Macabe had died.

It was a part of that strange summer that the death of the priest was like a stone flung into a stagnant pond from which the waves spread out across the whole peninsula. In the pubs of Kintillo, Toscaig and Camusrury, the patrons sat subdued, discussing the suddenness and terror of such a death. And while they drank their beer with whisky chasers, the women sat at home in the long evenings, knitting together in twos and threes and elaborating on the suffering of Father Macabe.

His body was taken away to be buried in Aberdeen and the shutters were closed on all the rectory windows that faced the bay. From the village below the house had a queer blank look like an idiot face that is crazed with grief and when the long twilight began, it shone strangely in the dusk and could still be seen long after the shoulder of the hill behind it had melted into the night.

11

Inside the rectory, now that the priest was dead, his housekeeper ate and slept when she pleased. Often she did not bother to get dressed. She walked about the darkened rooms in an old overcoat that she wore as a dressing gown and when she was hungry she made herself cups of sweet tea and cut slices from a Dundee cake that she had bought for Father Macabe before he died. She kept the kitchen range stoked up with fuel and she sat by the kitchen table stirring the cups of tea until they were almost cold. Occasionally a tea leaf floated to the top of the cup and she fished it out with a spoon and slapped it against the back of her hand, counting the days until a handsome stranger came to the door. Whenever she thought of the handsome stranger she began to laugh and the sound of this laughter was high and disconnected in the silence of the house.

She took leisurely walks about the house watching the dust build up on the woodwork and dropping the crumbs of her Dundee cake on the bare floorboards. The dust floated up and down the sunbeams between the shutters and settled on the furniture — she watched its progress from day to day — and still there was no sign of the new parish priest.

From the kitchen she looked out through the sycamore trees towards the church. Close to the kitchen window the parish car was parked. It was so old and dilapidated that some day it would break down on the steep flanks of the pass and refuse to move again. At such a thought Morag would smile to herself.

Twice she heard the church bell ringing for mass on a Sunday morning and twice she was dressed and sitting at the kitchen table waiting for Father Lanni to come to the rectory door. She would sit there without moving for almost an hour until she heard the congregation leaving the church at the end of mass. Then she would get up from her chair and open the shutter a little to watch for the priest coming out of the church. For two Sundays Father Lanni came down the cinder path from the vestry in a great hurry and climbed into his car without once glancing towards the rectory. Miss Morag closed the shutter again and celebrated those Sundays with a helping of extra food. By the third week, however, there was a single handful of dusty lentils at the bottom of a sack and the last of the porridge oats simmered in a pot on the range. There were even times in the dark silence of the empty house when she felt sure that the new priest would never come. On those days she strolled about freely, humming a certain tuneless song, and she would help herself to the drink that was locked in a cupboard under the stairs.

She was sitting one afternoon in Father Macabe's chair by the study fire staring at the sunlight through the shutters — shutting first one eye hard and then the other she saw the light jump sharply across the lino floor. She had a glass of sherry balanced on the arm of the chair and she was raising the remains to her mouth when the front door bell rang. She stopped with the glass half way to her lips and waited for it to ring again.

Father Lanni began to beat on the rectory door with his fist and to rattle the door knob. As soon as her brain started working again Miss Morag was out of her chair with great speed. She hid the sherry glass behind the coal scuttle, tightened the belt of her overcoat sharply and reached the front door just as Father Lanni had his finger on the bell for the second time.

'Ah Miss Morag?' he said, 'I was beginning to think the bell was out of order.' He stopped and stared at her. She was blinking in the sudden light and her face was pale and dirty. 'Are you ill?' he said. 'Is anything the matter with you?'

'You'll be wanting to come in then,' she said. She moved back in the shadows of the hall. 'I'll have to fix the shutters.'

14

She went ahead of him through the study door, and, while he hesitated in the unaccustomed darkness, she had time to hide the sherry bottle behind the big armchair before throwing the shutters back with a clatter against the walls.

'I haven't time to stay long,' Father Lanni said, 'I was up administering the last rites to Mrs Mackenzie at the Dower Farm.' He sat down with a sigh in Father Macabe's armchair and wiped his forehead with the back of his hand. 'I could do with a little refreshment,' he said. 'With my weight I suffer greatly from the heat.'

Miss Morag watched him with her arms folded and her back to the light. 'There's no much in the house,' she said without moving. 'The rations is all used up.'

She disliked Father Lanni for two reasons. He spoke slowly to her as if he were dealing with a backward child and, while some people ignored her wall eye or looked away, Father Lanni made an effort to stare her in the face in the same bold way he might have stared at a hunchback, to show that he was not afraid. 'Now Miss Morag,' he said playfully, 'considering I have come up here to the rectory to see how you're getting on, I think I'm entitled to a cup of tea.'

'As you wish,' she said shrugging. The light

15

hurt her eyes — it pressed down on the lids and made her dizzy. 'I'll away and make it then,' she said.

Father Lanni lay back in the chair with a yawn and when she came in with the tea tray his mouth was half open and his hands were folded loosely on his heavy stomach.

'There's no milk,' she said setting down the tray.

Father Lanni straightened himself up and sighed. 'Now look here, my good woman,' he said pouring out the tea, 'you will have to pull yourself together a bit before Father James arrives. Considering there are many people who would like a nice comfortable job like this . . . ' He put three lumps of sugar in the cup and stirred it thoroughly. 'It won't do,' he continued 'You have a nice respectable position here. Father James is a young man. He will certainly like things nicely done. He comes from the south, you understand, from England and they are very particular there about cleanliness and so forth . . . '

'Father James,' she said, 'that's a funny name.' She stood in front of the old priest with her arms folded and a sour expression on her face. 'It's a funny name,' she said again.

Father Lanni shook his head and made a clicking noise with his tongue. He finished his

16

tea in a hurry. The atmosphere in the room was warm and stale and the dust in his nostrils gave him an urge to sneeze. 'Now you're thinking about what I said.' He pulled himself slowly out of the chair and straightened the creases in his cassock. 'It's your Christian duty to have the place cleaned up and ready within the week.' By the study door he turned and looked at her severely. 'It was a beautiful mass we had last Sunday for Father Macabe. I was disappointed not to see you there, Miss Morag.'

For a moment she looked afraid. She pulled the old overcoat tightly round her body, and cradled herself with her bony hands. 'I couldn't go,' she said. 'I was sick.'

He looked at her a little longer and then he sighed and spoke carefully separating each word from the next. 'I am bringing Father James from the three o'clock train next Tuesday. We shall be here about five. I should like everything ready for him, you understand, otherwise . . . I shall have to take steps,' he said firmly. 'I shall have to speak to the bishop.'

He watched her while she took this item in. She ran her tongue over her lips and shifted her disconcerting gaze to the floor. 'It'll be done,' she said nodding. 'He won't need to complain.'

She saw that he was satisfied with that. He turned and went out into the hall fussing with the belt of his cassock and preparing himself to face the heat again. Miss Morag watched him from the shadows when he climbed into his car. She slammed the door behind him and waited until she heard him drive away. Then she walked into the study and smashed his tea cup on the floor. She stamped on the broken cup and when it was shattered into small fragments she went slowly to the kitchen and fetched a dustpan and brush. She swept up the pieces carefully and sponged down the lino floor and by the time the sun had set that evening she had cleaned out every room: she had polished the furniture, and dusted all the pictures and, finally, she opened the shutters and the windows wide. The sounds of the warm night came drifting back from the valley and the hillside and these sounds tormented her like the pieces of a half-heard song that she could no longer put together.

Morag was wall-eyed and ugly and the hair grew on her head in thin irregular tufts which resembled the down on a new born baby's scalp. Throughout the peninsula she was treated as a harmless joke. There was a certain ballad, sung late in the pubs, to the beating of fists upon the bar. It began with the legend of Morag's mother, Roving Mary, and of the unknown sailor who had fathered her sixty years before. And various verses were added to it from one year to the next. It was known throughout the peninsula as the the Ballad of Morag Anon. There were certain odd gaps in it where the singers had forgotten the facts, and sometimes an incident was invented to add more interest to it. For the truth of Morag's life was simple, uneventful and often sad.

Roving Mary was sent away from Kintillo and Lady Finlay brought up her daughter to be kitchen maid in her place. She was dressed in cast-off clothes and sent to the village school where she neither learned to read nor write, and she grew up to peel potatoes and sweep out the kitchens of Kintillo House. She scoured the range and took the pails of pig-swill down to the home farm, and when her work was done, she would sit dumbly in a chair for hours at a time, and her odd eyes would flitter about the room like restless birds that had nowhere to alight.

Succeeding cooks complained about her, saying that she worked too slowly and without any system, so that when she was nearly thirty, Lady Finlay took her up the road to the rectory where the post of housekeeper had fallen vacant. She never left again. For a long time she worked with a dim sadness that settled over everything she did. As she looked from the study window, out across the bay, her eyes would fill with tears though she had no idea what she was crying for.

When Father Macabe came to Kintillo he treated her kindly. He listened when she spoke to him and he never finished a sentence for her, nor hurried her through one. The little religion she had scraped together was lifted from his sermons on a Sunday morning. She fell in love with him and this love was like an unaccustomed warmth after a long winter, that spread throughout her body and gave a peculiar brightness to her one blue eye.

One day Father Macabe asked her to come into the study and sit across from him in an armchair. He had never done this before and Morag sat down uneasily and gazed at the floor in front of her. While the priest was speaking she became more and more absorbed by the pattern in the carpet which stretched between them. And afterwards she could only think of his coming death clearly when she remembered its ugly floral design, as if the greater of the two realities was this.

For the next three days she stayed in her room and the priest had to cook for himself.

Occasionally he leaned against her door and asked her to come out, altering the tone of his voice in various ways to try and move her. When he listened closely he heard nothing, but at night when he lay in bed he could hear through the walls a high thin keening like the howling of an animal whose master has left it. When her elected time of mourning was over, Morag never cried again, not even on the day he died. And when the undertakers came, she looked indifferently at his corpse before it was put into the coffin. Then she walked across the passage to her room.

In a box there, she kept a few things that he had given her — a wooden rosary, a child's prayer book and some postcards that he had sent her from Aberdeen. Sometimes, when her memories of him became vague or confused, she would open this box and run her hands lightly over the objects inside it. In this way she was able to remember again exactly how he was.

She hated the new priest with a profound intensity. She hated him some time before she had ever met him.

2

'And it won't be easy,' Father Lanni was saying again. 'I'm afraid it won't be easy at all.'

'I didn't expect . . . '

'And the thing you have to remember — have some more tea — is that these people are scarcely Christian. Consider the mission of Saint Iona in the fourth century. Large parts of this coast were converted to Catholicism and many of them have remained so ever since, but do you think this is out of a sense of conviction?'

'Yes, I believe they . . . '

'Well it's nothing of the sort. If the Protestant reformers had made an effort to reach these coasts they could have converted whole areas to the Church of Scotland. The religion here is entirely superficial — basically they are all pagans, complete pagans.'

Father James let him talk. Since he had arrived half an hour ago in the rectory and indeed since he had left the station in Fort William the new priest had scarcely been able to open his mouth. Father Lanni had lived so long alone that it was impossible for him to listen to anyone else without becoming restless and uneasy.

'. . . They are pagan by character, you see, as well as by tradition. Because they live mostly from the land and above all from the sea, the seasons, the climate — these things affect them far more than anything we can impose upon them in the way of discipline — basically, you see . . .'

While he was talking Father James murmured and nodded now and then, and looked about the room. The rectory study was small and dark, overshadowed by the trees outside the window: from where he sat he could see nothing but the sky imprisoned there and a small patch of leaves moving silently in the slight wind, up and down the same window pane. Inside the room the paint on the walls had turned yellow with age and the woodwork was varnished brown. There were patches of damp around the skirting boards and in the corners of the ceiling. And all these things, even the worn-out lino and the dingy rug in front of the fireplace, were identical to the rectory he had left five hours ago in Lennoxtown.

Father Lanni was finishing the buttered bread and filling up the tea pot again. '. . . and there was another thing I meant to discuss with you which I almost forgot . . . I daresay you have been worrying about Miss Morag, the housekeeper . . . '

Father James smiled. 'Not at all. She seems perfect. No one will gossip about us, will they, up here on the hill together alone?'

'I don't think you take my point,' Father Lanni said heavily. 'I daresay you haven't had time to notice her, well, her manner.'

'Oh yes,' said Father James gently, 'I should imagine she's quite simple-minded, but that doesn't worry me, you know. We shan't see very much of each other and I'm sure she does her work very well or she . . . '

'Yes, well, if it really doesn't worry you.'

Father Lanni was uneasy. He felt that the conversation was only half finished; there were essential points in it that he hadn't developed yet. But Father James had a curious way of speaking that was light and at the same time solemn. The old priest couldn't pin it down. If he had been able to put it into words he would have said that he resembled a man who is pursuing a certain dream in which both the time and the place had been chosen long ago. He sat for a little in silence and stirred his cup of tea, while Father James sat watching him.

'Have you been here long at Dornie?'

'Yes, a long time now . . . a very long time. I took over the parish there at the same time that Father Macabe came here.'

'You must miss him then . . . I'm sorry.'

'I miss his company,' said Father Lanni. He felt the return of an old grievance. 'You don't get much civilized company round here. They're a lazy lot — no interest in anything, you see, no curiosity, I mean intellectual curiosity you understand. Most of them are quite content to live out their lives catching a few fish, poaching salmon, growing a few turnips and potatoes and of course drinking . . . '

'They must be very poor.'

'Poor? They don't try. Do you realize no one has made the slightest effort to drain the land . . . apart from the valley of course? There are whole acres of the hillside around here that could be planted up with trees. Forestry brings in a nice income. But no one does a thing. I am constantly exhorting them from the pulpit — there are plenty of examples throughout the country of flourishing communities, growing populations and so forth under exactly the same conditions . . . '

'But surely it's the landowner's . . . '

'Under exactly the same conditions . . . and if you think I haven't told them. But it's always the same. They complain that the population is decreasing and I tell them over and over again if only . . . but it's no use talking.' Father Lanni tugged angrily at his dog collar and rose suddenly to his feet. 'Here,' he said, 'I'll show you . . . Come outside a minute . . . ' He took the young priest by the arm and dragged him to the door. 'I'll show you what I mean,' he said. 'I'll show you just what I mean.'

Outside a warm south wind was blowing across the valley and the air was full of light. Father James shut his eyes and let the sun shine full in his face. On his own he might have walked down to the beach for a while where the tide was going out and the sands stretched clear to the mouth of the bay. But Father Lanni was still holding on to him, and was shouting in his ear.

' . . . and over there,' he was saying pointing up the hillside, 'is a perfect example . . . wasted land . . . two hundred acres at least . . . completely going to waste . . . '

The wind blew his voice away and Father James was no longer listening. He looked down across the bay. The village of Kintillo faced north among the hollows of Ben Beann. There was a line of white cottages above the beach, a high wood, a few fields and a one-track road going south to Camusrury and Toscaig. The mountains of Torridon rose up in a circle to the north and east, and to the west, across the sea, the ragged lines of the Cuillins were black against the evening sky.

' . . . and do you realize,' cried Father Lanni, 'you can't even grow runner beans here? And do you know why not? The light, there's not enough light. In the winter after two o'clock in the afternoon it's dark, completely dark.' While he spoke his face was now so close to Father James' that a gob of spit hit the young priest on the cheek. 'I think we'd better go in,' he said gloomily. 'It's almost time for supper. Though considering the kind of food . . . '

He released Father James' arm at last and they went back into the house. 'It will certainly be mutton,' he said as they sat down for the evening meal. He spread out his napkin carefully on his knees. 'I can guarantee it'll be mutton. When I think eight years back . . . to the time I arrived in Dornie, we used to get good meat then, straight from the local markets . . . rump steak, wing rib, even occasionally a nice leg of pork . . . and now what do you think they cook? Scotch broth . . . lentil soup . . . mashed turnips. When I think . . . There, you see? Good evening Miss Morag, that looks delicious.'

Miss Morag came in with a bowl of brown soup and pushed the door shut with her bottom. She nodded at the priests, put down the plates and soup tureen on the side table, and left.

'After you,' said Father Lanni. 'You must do the honours . . . considering that this is now your parish.'

Father James smiled absent-mindedly. He felt unable to make any effort. His head had begun to ache and he felt very tired. Nothing was the way he had imagined it. He had thought about this place for so long, planned what he would do and prayed for it. And now that he was there he felt only exhaustion. The old priest's conversation tightened around him like a web: there were hundreds of invisible threads which tied him down and prevented him from thinking clearly about anything. He kept saying to himself, 'I have done nothing. I have been here for three hours and I have done nothing.' He suddenly realized that he had eaten half his meal without seeing or tasting a single mouthful. Father Lanni was leaning forward asking him something. He was rolling up pieces of bread in his thick fingers and the crumbs were scattered round his plate.

' . . . and you won't mind me saying this I hope — I mean since we've only just met.'

'I'm sorry. I wasn't listening. What was it?'

'But they aren't — I mean the parish

— they won't be expecting you . . . someone like you, you see . . . '

Father James was surprised. 'I don't understand. I'm just an ordinary parish priest. From what you said I thought they weren't really interested in me.'

Father Lanni swayed anxiously in his chair. 'No, no, you misunderstood me. No, these things affect them deeply. I mean, changes in the community . . . such a small enclosed community as this. No, they are vitally concerned, you see, but the thing is . . . I don't know how to put it . . . '

'Because I'm English, you mean, they might find me odd? Perhaps they won't understand the way I speak. Do they resent the English?'

'Oh, no, no, no! Not that! Well, perhaps a little, but no . . . ' The old man became agitated. Crumbs bounced off his cassock and he flapped at them with clumsy fingers. The expression on his face was at once sly and embarrassed. 'Forgive me Father James,' he said leaning forward in his chair, 'but you look, well you see, for this kind of parish . . . Now you won't take offence will you? You see, you are too young and really too er . . . different.' He was disconcerted. Father James began to laugh. The knife and fork he was holding slipped from his hands and fell

29

on the floor. He bent to pick them up, and afterwards his face was flushed with embarrassment.

'I'm sorry,' he said, 'I didn't mean to laugh. That was rude of me. But you reminded me of my Father Administrator. He gave me the same warning just a little while ago. He was very against my coming here. I think, if there had been anyone else he could have sent, I should never have been considered. He warned me against the isolation and the loneliness. He said that I shouldn't last out the year in such a place.' He smiled. 'But it was the way he speaks, like a man rewriting the Bible. He said, 'Small flocks have sharp eyes.' I think that was just what you meant, wasn't it?'

'Well yes — in effect — yes.'

Father Lanni was now uncomfortable. He became shy and vague. 'Yes, well . . . it won't be easy for you then. You see, they will be naturally suspicious. For this reason it won't be easy.' He shook his head slowly. He was conscious of coming round in a full circle upon himself. 'Tell me about your last parish,' he said suddenly.

They ate trifle from little glass dishes that were chipped and grey. The trifle was pasty and insipid but Father Lanni finished his rapidly and licked the spoon until it was clean. 'I gather you had no holiday between these two posts?'

'No. Things happened in the end so quickly, there was no time. I wish, in a way, that I had. I should have liked to go home for a while. I come from a large family, you know. So much seems to happen there without being organized and I love that — the noise and the chaos — I'm used to it. The dogs cover the sofas with hair, the rabbits escape from their hutches and nest in the drawing room and sometimes,' he said laughing, 'we have no joint for Sunday lunches — the dogs get into the larder and eat it.'

Father Lanni laughed too but he stopped almost immediately. 'I'm afraid you will find it very dull here,' he said repressively, 'very dull indeed.'

'Oh no,' Father James said, leaning forward quickly. 'You don't understand, I want . . . '

But what it was he wanted he never said — suddenly he stopped speaking and flushed. When he flushed his eyes watered with embarrassment. He had eyes of a deep strong blue, the lids heavy and finely shaped and the eyelashes long and curved, and when he was excited the irises darkened until they were almost black and they shone with a strange intensity. The old man pursed his lips and

31

sighed. Certainly, Father James had never been troubled by loneliness in his life. Fresh from a university or a seminary — it made no difference — he was the same bright-faced and hopeless idealist that Father Lanni had often seen before.

'I'm sorry,' Father James was saying, 'it's very difficult for me to explain why I wanted to come here. You see, to do that I would have to . . . it's very personal . . . it's part of a . . . ' He meant to say 'a dream' but once again he stopped himself, sighed and began again. 'I was going to tell you about my last parish, wasn't I?' He smiled and this smile lit up the whole of his face.

'Oh he has charm,' Father Lanni thought. 'Oh he has that all right. But it's the wrong kind of behaviour for this place. He's an intellectual — imagine sending an intellectual like that here.' 'Lennoxtown wasn't it?' he said aloud. 'A very large busy parish, that. I haven't been down to that part of Scotland recently. Glasgow I know, you understand . . . but Lennoxtown, I never had the opportunity of going there . . . a very prosperous busy parish I've heard though, plenty going on and so forth.'

'Well yes . . . ' said Father James politely, 'I suppose some of the things we managed to get done, but on the whole I thought the place was so poor, I wondered how we should . . . '

'Poor!' Father Lanni cried. 'You should see the squalor that some of the people round here live in — not fit for pigs mind you — and do you think I can get them to take an interest or a pride in themselves, considering the time I have spent?'

Father James pressed his hands hard together in his lap. It was useless to argue. Everything returned to the same point. Like a merry-go-round at a fair the conversation went up and down, up and down, but always in the same circle and at the same speed. He remembered his first few days in Lennox-town, his first parish. He had been so proud, so full of enthusiasm, he had walked from one end of the town to the other and found every street the same. The air was bitter from the smell of the tanning factory and a constant wind blew around the corners, a sad wind from the Campsie fells, full of grit and empty paper bags. The town was empty — there was nothing to do there — and the mods and rockers polished their motor bikes and drove off to Glasgow on Saturday nights where the poverty was noisy and real and the streets were neon lit. He had done nothing there — nothing that he really wanted to do.

'Perhaps we should go next door,' he said,

getting to his feet. 'I didn't realize how late it was getting. I still haven't unpacked yet or done anything.'

'Ah yes,' said Father Lanni, 'one forgets, what with the long twilights we get here.' He folded up his napkin and rose from the table, staggering a little under his own weight. In the narrow hallway, practically pressed against Father Lanni's stomach, the young priest said good night.

'I hope you'll forgive me,' he said. 'I have so much to do upstairs. I think I should get everything sorted out — my books and things.'

'Go ahead, my son, I understand,' Father Lanni said. He ran a finger round the inside of his mouth where a piece of food was lodged. 'I shall go to bed myself soon. I don't sit around very late in the evenings as a rule . . . '

Father James watched him go slowly into the study. He felt guilty. There were many evenings which the old man must have spent by the fireside with Father Macabe. And on those evenings there had been someone to listen to him while he talked, a little drink to warm him before he went to bed, and the sound of someone moving about in another room when he turned out the light to go to sleep. 'I should go in there and sit with him again,' he thought. He shut his eyes and leaned against the cool bannisters. Somewhere at the base of his skull, a headache was spreading out, like the tendrils of some poisonous plant which prevented him from thinking of anything clearly. 'I must go and unpack,' he said aloud, but almost immediately he changed his mind. He opened the front door quietly and walked out into the night.

The days in Kintillo are long and wax-yellow in midsummer and you can read a book out of doors until eleven o'clock on a warm evening. The stillness is so complete that if a child cries out or a door slams across the water, in the village it can be clearly heard from the rectory garden and it leaves a space behind it in the night. Father James walked up the shoulder of the hill on a little path which ran through the trees behind the house. He walked quickly and noiselessly. Half way up the hill, however, he stumbled on a sharp piece of rock and a few stones rattled loose down the steep slope behind him. He turned round quickly as though he expected to see Father Lanni come out from the shadows of the house and look up the hill towards him. There was nothing. The silence was so deep that he could hear the sound of his own breathing. Then he noticed in a back window on the first floor of the rectory there was a face pressed against the window pane, staring directly towards him in the dusk. He had the strange impression that Miss Morag had watched him, motionless, since he left the house and that she would go on staring at him with the same terrible attentiveness until he was out of sight over the lip of the hill.

He walked on until he lost the path among some rocks and the rectory was far below him in the hollow. He was quite alone on the bare mountainside. Above him the ground stretched up to a sharp skyline and beyond it on the other side he knew there was nothing for thirty-five miles along the coast but the ruins of deserted crofts and the empty wastes of the moors. Down in the bay the sea was calm and the tiny village of Kintillo hung to the far shore like a cluster of pebbles that sooner or later the tide will wash away. He sat for a long time on the shoulder of the hill, watching the light fade and thicken on the water and the shadows change slowly from grey to black.

Ten years ago on a similar night in summer, he had decided to become a priest. But the nights in the south of England had a different feeling to them. Although the splendour was missing from them, in its place there were the numberless soft sounds: the stirring of leaves and grass, and the movement of a small night world along the hedges and in the woods around his house. And down by the river while he was fishing, the sky was a pale apple green by half past eight and dark by nine o'clock.

He could no longer remember when the idea to become a priest had first occurred to him, and for a while he had ignored it. He would get up in the mornings thinking, 'There is something disagreeable I have to do today' and then he would remember what it was. For the spring of one year and half the summer, he refused to give in to it. He had been in love with his cousin Alice, and this love was absurd and painful. He watched her and could not touch her. He was tormented by her indifference and yet there was something delightful about this torment. It was intolerable that he should be asked to give it up. To give it up, moreover, for a life of chastity and uncompromising belief which was cold and repulsive to him.

He went to France, in the beginning of that July, with his brother Michael and a friend and when they reached Paris, they decided to stay there instead of going on to the Auvergne as they planned to do. For ten days and nights they wasted their money among the bars and small nightclubs on the Left Bank.

Frequently they ate nothing in the mornings, nor at lunch time either, so that this money could be spent on cheap wine, small dingy floor shows and finally on prostitutes. These experiences were some of them delightful and others, for no reason, pointless and sad. And presently they began to find — each of them without telling the others — that whole evenings had passed which they could not remember. It was as if they had paid their money at the door to see some show and had walked instead into some strange uneasy darkness.

Two days after he came home, he went down to the river to fish. He had two things on his mind. First there was his faithlessness to his cousin Alice which he now considered with a certain guilty pleasure and then there was another feeling which he could not put into words. For a long time now he had been in a state of indecision. He would decide to become a lawyer one day and then a teacher the next. Or he would decide he was going to university, and then gradually forget the idea, finding it a waste of time. He would begin to study something that interested him, collect together any number of books on the subject, but when the time came for him to start on this, he would abandon the whole idea and go out to some party instead. Finally that evening by the river bank, while he was standing there half-hypnotized by the water's movements, he saw clearly that all these fine thoughts and ideals amounted to as little as a row of beans.

He was eighteen. He had time to make up his mind what he wanted to do. But the idea was already there and not merely there but clear to him in every detail. Almost with relief, he had returned to it and was surprised to discover that somehow it suited him. Going home through the dark fields he walked slowly and was almost in a dream. Once he said to himself aloud, 'I'm going to become a priest' and immediately he smiled, for the words no longer sounded strange to him.

Father James gazed out across the bay. Ben Beann was still visible against the night sky and beyond it the clear lines of the coast spread out to the south, one dark ridge after another going down into the sea. Although his eyes took in these things, in his mind he could see another valley, the broad valley of the Thames, the streets of a busy city and the pale stone cloisters of the Oxford seminary. He had spent seven years in Oxford and now those years had shortened themselves into a single memory of intense happiness.

Suddenly a bird cried out behind him on

the hill. He realized that he was cold and that the night had finally come. He got up stiffly from the rock he had been sitting on and started back down the path again towards the rectory.

3

When he came down the next morning Father Lanni was already eating breakfast. He was finishing a boiled egg. In spite of the clean way he had cut off the top of it and in spite of the napkin tucked into his collar, he had managed to spill some yolk on the cuff of his cassock.

'Good morning to you,' he said as the new priest came in. 'I hope you slept well, my son. It's a strange thing though, considering that I like to get about a bit and have a change now and then, I can never sleep well in an unfamiliar room . . . and then of course, though I don't mean to depress you . . . the food here . . . I had terrible indigestion last night.'

While he was getting dressed, Father James had thought of a number of things to ask the old priest about his new parish. But now when he sat down opposite him and began to eat his breakfast, he found that he had forgotten half of them and the rest seemed scarcely worth mentioning. He poured himself a cup of tea.

'It's another beautiful day again,' he said.

'This weather is unnatural, however,' said Father Lanni. 'You know we are having a drought here.'

'Yes, I did hear something about it. I heard there might have to be some kind of water rationing.'

'Huh, well that kind of thing will never get organized round here. Such a notion is completely foreign to these people. Economy is something they have never understood; they are born wasters.'

Father James interrupted him quickly. 'I know what I wanted to ask you,' he said. 'I was wondering if you could go through the parish register with me. I was hoping you might be able to sort out the various families a little. For instance, I know there are a great number of Mackenzies and also Macleods. Perhaps with your help I should get a better feeling of the place.'

Father Lanni was gazing at him again with a faded stare. 'Well,' he said, 'I haven't much time . . . '

'Oh I know, I do appreciate . . . '

'Not at all. I don't get much civilized company. It's a real pleasure to be here but I must get back to my parish duties and so forth — you know how it is, when you leave other people to do the work it never gets done — so the simplest thing would be, when you've finished your breakfast . . . '

'I'm ready now.'

'Yes, well, the simplest thing would be if I take you down to the village now on my way home. I know they are anxious to see what . . . to meet you, you see, and then I really must be getting on home.'

As they were leaving the house the telephone rang and Miss Morag came out of the study. Without looking at Father James she said, 'It's for you, then.'

'For me?' he asked. He felt the blood rising in his face. Miss Morag went through the baize door into the kitchen without replying.

'It'll be Mr Finlay,' Father Lanni whispered suddenly in his ear.

'Who?'

'The son of the Laird. You'd better go in there and speak to him quickly.'

Two minutes later Father James came back. 'He's asked me to dinner,' he said.

'That's wonderful news,' Father Lanni cried, 'wonderful news. I was sure he would ask you. Father Macabe always dined there on Sunday nights.'

'What is he like? I'm afraid I must have made a bad impression on him. He was very cold and abrupt.'

'Mr Finlay?' the old man said vaguely. He was at a loss to describe him. 'Well now, his

43

life has not been easy you see, but considering this, he is a wonderful man . . . very educated and quite devoted to his father of course . . . ' Charles Finlay existed in his mind in the same way as a river flows down its natural course and the sun sets in the same place on the horizon. As they walked out to his car he elaborated instead on the long and noble history of the Finlays: how it was that they had lived on the same land for four or even five centuries and how they had bravely fought the English at the battle of Culloden Moor. While they drove down the hill towards the village he indicated the size and grandeur of their Georgian house with a sweep of his hand and the old car ran over a stone in the road and swerved about. He pointed out the lodge gates through which it was believed the ghost of General Robert Finlay drove with his coach and four, on moonless nights, when the Lairds of Kintillo lay dying, and Father James gazed distract-edly at the spot of dried egg on the cuff of his cassock.

Suddenly Father Lanni stopped the car in the middle of the road and climbed out. He leaned over the edge of the door. 'It's a terrible business to turn round on the sea road once you are on it. I prefer to leave my car here where it's ready to go up the pass.'

'Is it all right — in the middle of the road I mean?'

'Nothing goes up this road,' Father Lanni said simply. 'You might say it's now your exclusive property. The North Lodge gates are never used, you understand. The old man, Sir John, does not go visiting now that his wife is dead — there is no occasion to keep up the grandeur of the past.'

They began to walk up the road to the village. The wind had veered to the west and Father Lanni's cassock billowed out gently behind him like a boat that has half caught sail. 'My, my,' he said, 'what beautiful weather we're having. I think I can see Angus Cameron in the village street idling around as usual — a perfect example of what I was telling you now about the laziness of these people — he's twenty-six, able-bodied, perfectly intelligent and yet I don't believe he has done a day's real work in his life.'

As the two priests walked up the village street, there was a long unnatural silence. By the sea wall, a man was mending an old Ford van. Around the upraised bonnet, though his hands were occupied, his eyes were fixed on the priests. Two children were playing beside him in the road. Their high voices broke off in mid air and they too began to stare. The silence was so complete that if one of the priests had dropped a coin in the road he would have heard it roll away into the ditch. Father James, with his very clear skin, began to blush and he felt his hands grow soft and damp. His black cloth suit cut him off from the village people and though Father Lanni greeted the children by name as he went past they answered him at random with their eyes on the new priest.

When they reached the post office, Father Lanni began talking loudly before he was halfway through the door as though this was a pre-arranged signal for the people inside to straighten themselves from lounging against the counter. The post office was dark and cramped and the air was dusty. Besides dealing with the mail the postmistress ran a general store. The wall behind the counter was stacked to the ceiling with sacks of lentils and flour, tin boxes of biscuits and crates of cheap soap which gave out a sour and bitter smell. The counter was crowded with jars of sweets, postcard racks, and bundles of pens and pencils tied up with elastic bands. In the middle of this confusion, like a single flower growing out of a rubbish heap, stood Jean Macpherson, the postmistress. She was sorting the letters beside her on the counter, stamping them and throwing them into a mailbag on the floor. She smiled shyly at the

46

priests and went on with her work.

'It's fine weather we're having,' said Father Lanni.

'It is that,' she answered. Her skin was very pale and there were freckles on the bridge of her nose.

'Father James came down the beach road with me,' he said, 'to see me on my way. I thought we'd take the opportunity to call in and see you while we were passing. I told Father James you'd look after him, Jeanie, if he has any problems, you see, with his mail and things.'

There were three other men in the shop planted among the shadows. They were shifting from one foot to another and staring at the wall behind the counter. At the mention of Father James they felt free to stare at him for a minute before returning their gazes again to the wall.

'I should be very grateful for your help,' Father James said to Jeanie. For some reason she blushed and began to fiddle with the letters in front of her on the counter. The shop was now so quiet that the sounds coming from another room could be clearly heard and seemed oddly loud and emphatic. 'The Reverend Father,' said the old priest, 'has been telling me how much he admires the scenery here.'

'It's your first visit then?' Jeanie spoke softly, so that Father James had to lean forward slightly to hear her.

'Yes. I've never been to the west coast before. I think it's very beautiful.'

One of the men behind him in the shadows cleared his throat. 'There was a fellow up here not long ago,' he began 'You remember him, Jean, from one of the big newspapers in the south. And this fellow came here for the weekend on his way north. He was so full of the place he stayed two weeks in the end.'

'I remember him,' she said. 'He sent me this cutting from the newspaper about Danny and the turtle he caught in the Minch. Wait now I have it here. I'll get it out if you're interested.'

'I should like to see that very much,' said Father James.

'A turtle in the Minch,' said Father Lanni. 'Most unusual — quite extraordinary I should say.' He peered at the yellow paper which was now in front of him. 'Ninety pounds. My goodness, that's a great size, isn't it?'

The three men also passed the picture from hand to hand, admiring it in the dim light, and turning it over for some reason to stare at the back.

The atmosphere had warmed a little, like

the first few sips of whisky on a cold night that are raw in the throat and spread out gently in the stomach afterwards. Jeanie Macpherson lifted up the flap of the post-office counter. 'Would you care for a cup of tea?' she said to the priests. 'Come in to the sitting room and m'mother'll make you one.'

'Well that's very kind of you,' Father James began, 'but we've just . . . '

'I'd be most grateful,' Father Lanni said firmly. 'We could do with a little refreshment.'

He walked round the edge of the counter into the dark little sitting room behind, where he settled himself in the one armchair, and Father James following behind sat on a stiff-backed chair by the window. The room faced north like the rest of the village and the smell of cheap soap followed them through the door as they sat and waited for their tea. Jeanie's mother came in from the kitchen and leant against the threshold staring at them.

'Good morning, Father Lanni,' she said. 'Say hello to the new father, children.' From somewhere among the folds of her apron two children dragged themselves free and ran away into the kitchen. 'They're only small,' she said.

'Are those your grandchildren?' said Father James.

'They're a fine looking pair, Mrs Mackay,' said Father Lanni. 'They're growing up fast.'

'They're cunning enough mind,' she said sighing. 'It was a lovely mass for the dead,' she went on. She spoke to Father Lanni but her eyes were fixed on the new priest. Steam came through the door from the kitchen and the kettle began to hiss on the range. 'I'll away and make the tea then,' she said shifting her weight reluctantly from the doorpost. She was back in a little while watching the two priests sit down to their second pot of tea of the morning. The biscuits were stale and tasted of dust, but Mrs Mackay waited in the doorway with her arms resting on her bosom until they had finished them.

'I think we must be going,' Father James said getting up. 'Thank you so much for the tea.'

'You're welcome.'

'How is Mr Finlay?' asked Father Lanni. The hot tea had brought out a film of damp on his forehead and upper lip. He wiped his face with a crumpled handkerchief.

'Mr Finlay? He's the same, the very same.'

'And Sir John?'

'Fair getting on — he's past ninety now. And with the heat . . . ' She shrugged and turned to the new priest. 'Drop in when you like, Father. We're always here.'

When he thanked her she dipped her head a little, shook herself free of the door frame again and went back into the kitchen. Before they were out of the sitting-room door Father James could see her beyond the kitchen in her small backyard, talking to a neighbour over the fence.

Father James said goodbye to the old priest by the fork in the road and watched him drive away. The light flashed once on the roof of the car and then it was gone into the darkness of the woods that lined the hill. Father James walked slowly along the beach. Halfway he turned round as if he hoped to see the old Morris coming back through the shadows of the trees that had swallowed it and bursting out again into the sunlight of the bay. Just a little while ago he had fretted to begin on things and now he walked idly along the lip of grass above the beach and could think of nothing whatsoever to do. The light weighed on his eyes and made them water and the midday heat confused him.

There was a sound of someone running down the hill, jumping the dried out ruts and spinning pebbles in the road. He looked up and saw a young girl coming towards him over the beach. She had a great mass of red hair blowing out around her face. She ran with her head thrown back to the sun and the skin of her arms and neck was a startling white. She was laughing, half blinded by the light and the rushing air, half balanced in the ancient dream that if she spread her arms she might float upwards on a current of the wind. When she saw the priest, she slowed down and stumbled in the road and then she walked on primly towards him, gathering up her hair that had shaken loose and tying it back to the nape of her neck. She was dressed in jeans and an Aertex shirt and on her feet she had a pair of flimsy sandals that flapped as she walked along — her toes were covered with dust from the road. She might have been any age from twelve to seventeen. Father James smiled and said good morning as he passed her but she bent her head without replying and he heard her start to run again as he went up the hill.

He worked hard for the rest of the day. He wrote letters and prepared his weekly sermon. He studied the parish register and checked the parish supplies. And finally he read his breviary and arranged his books on the study shelves.

When he went to bed that night, although it was still early, he felt very tired. He had only one clear memory of the day behind him and the rest of his impressions were vague and confused. Before he slept he thought briefly of the girl with the dark red hair, running down the road towards the beach.

4

It was extraordinary that his housekeeper chose Saturday morning to begin one of the few conversations with Father James that she was ever to have. As soon as he sat down to his breakfast, he spread out the sheets of his sermon beside him on a plate and began, for the third time that morning, to make certain he had memorized it.

'The daughters is home,' Miss Morag said.

Father James sighed and put down his knife and fork. The bacon was crisp and the egg yolks a rich creamy yellow. Miss Morag stood over him and prevented him from enjoying them. 'The daughters?' he said. 'Whose daughters?'

'His — down the road,' she said jerking her head towards the south window.

'Mr Finlay? But he hasn't any daughters.'

'He has — two of them. Back for the holidays once a year. An aunt has them in the meantime.'

'But no one's spoken to me about them.'

'Not to yous they wouldn't.'

Father James looked up. With one eye Miss Morag was watching him and the other travelled in little jumps on the wall above his head. 'What do you mean?' he said. 'I don't understand you.'

'Theys two beauties Father, and you such a good-looking young priest.' She laughed and closed one eye and the effect of this was suddenly frightening. Father James, staring up at her from his chair was certain for a moment that she was neither simple-minded nor insane. It was like gazing through the window of a deserted house and seeing there for a second that a face stared back at him — moreover a face that was malicious and perfectly intelligent. When she opened her other eye the feeling of horror left him and he looked away. 'You's a nice-looking man,' she said and laughed again.

Father James rose suddenly from his chair. He was a foot and a half taller than Miss Morag. While he spoke she listened to the tone of his voice and stared without blinking at the floor. 'I think you had better go and find something to do in the kitchen,' he said. 'I think you had better leave me to finish my breakfast in peace.'

Miss Morag started towards the door, putting as much space between herself and the priest as she could manage in the narrow room. She went sideways along the edge of the table and made a scuttling rush for the door. Before she shut it behind her, she made certain that the priest had sat down again with his back to her and was eating the remains of a fried egg. She put out her tongue and drove her eyes towards the bridge of her nose in a terrible squint, and then she softly shut the door.

★ ★ ★

That same Sunday, Father James went down the road to dinner with the Finlays. As he walked up the drive through the North Lodge Gates he heard the Kintillo river running through the thick woods to his left, faint and milky in the drought. Above this and almost drowning the sound entirely, was the noise of rooks coming home to roost in the trees above his head. Their nests hung thick and close together, and in the winter they crusted the trees like black spots where the sap had oozed out and formed ugly growths on the branches. Rhododendrons grew wild along the drive, and at their roots there was a soft bitter smell of moss and rotting undergrowth.

Half a mile along this drive the woods to one side fell away and Father James saw the house, set deep in the middle of the valley, facing west towards the Inner Sound and the cliffs of Raasay beyond. It was cut off like an

56

island in the centre of its park, between the river on one side and the high shoulder of the hill on the other. Its isolated position gave the house a strange, sad grandeur; and because the late sun shone full on the west front, the windows were blank with light, and the place had the queer shuttered look of a deserted building.

Father James walked up a flight of stone steps and rang the bell. While he waited he looked out across the park. The sun rested just above a rim of trees by the far sea wall and the shadows of these trees sprang back almost the full length of the park to the edge of the gravel before the house.

A young girl let him into the hall. She wore a long wool dress and her blonde hair fell in a fine loose sweep to her shoulders. The hall was cold and dark. After the sunlight of the bay, he could make out nothing in that huge space but the white moonface of a grandfather clock and a number of stags' heads in rows going up the walls. He crossed the hall carefully, afraid to knock into the umbrella stand or the rows of boots, whose shapes he could feel around him in the shadows. The girl was waiting for him by a great mahogany door. 'In here, Father,' she said. 'Come in.'

At that moment the grandfather clock beside him struck eight, and the priest was so distracted by the noise that he tripped over a piece of the study carpet as he was going through the door. The carpet stretched from one end of the room to the other. It was so worn that patches all over its surface had come unsewn; the whole effect in the late evening sun was of a roughly ploughed field. It was on one of these unsewn patches that Father James now stumbled and at the same time he knocked an ashtray from a pie crust table on to the floor. He spent a few minutes searching for the ashtray under the sofa and rearranging it on the table and when he straightened up, his eyes were watering with embarrassment.

The young girl asked him what he would like to drink — whisky or sherry. She gathered up her skirt and stepped neatly over the gaps in the carpet. She handed the priest a whisky and soda and threw a log on the fire. The sparks flew up demented from its damp. In spite of the west sun that came through the windows, the air in the room was cold and a great fire burned in the grate. She picked up a silver bowl and said, 'Have some cashew nuts. Take as many as you like — there are plenty more.'

The priest said, 'Thank you, I'm afraid I've arrived too early.'

She reassured him, saying that it was the

maid's night off. Her grandfather took some getting into his wheelchair. He was heavy and last summer he had fallen out of the chair one day on to the stone floor and had broken his hip.

Father James went to the window and remarked that the view from there across the sound was very beautiful.

The girl agreed. It was one of the most beautiful views on the entire west coast from those windows of the house. She ran one hand through the thick strands of her hair and let them fall again to her neck. She said wasn't the Aubusson carpet beautiful — it was insured for several thousand pounds — and then she blushed remembering that Father James had tripped over it coming into the room. The priest took some cashew nuts, putting them into his mouth one by one, passing the time.

'I think I can hear my father coming now.' She stood up, and shook out the folds of her skirt as though dust had gathered there. The door opened and Charles Finlay wheeled his father into the room. The old man sat placidly with his hands folded in his lap. There was a tartan rug around his knees and his shoulders were covered with a shawl.

There are certain scenes which remain in the mind as if they are meant to be taken in and referred to a long time afterwards. Charles Finlay seemed to search out the priest's eyes and there was something awkward and painful about this stare which made Father James look away. His eyes were curiously dense and cold, like certain stones that are flawed and hold the light unevenly. They were of a remarkable blue and there was no expression in them whatsoever.

Finlay said, 'This is my father, Sir John.' He bent over the wheelchair and said distinctly, 'This is the new priest, Papa, Father James.'

'Father Macabe?'

'No, this is Father James. Father Macabe is dead.'

The old man said nothing. One hand twitched in his lap and he closed the palm of the other over it in a rigid grip.

'Er — Anne you've already met.' Charles Finlay looked at his watch. 'Meriel should be here. She's late.'

The old man said loudly, 'Where is Meriel? I can't see her. Is she there?'

Someone spoke softly from the doorway. 'I'm here, grandpapa.'

'You're late,' Finlay said. He looked at his watch again. 'You're twenty minutes late.'

Meriel Finlay stood in the shadows of the great mahogany door. Her hand was still on the door knob as if by letting go of it she would have fallen into that terrible stretch of space that separated her from the rest of them. As she crossed the floor the blood rose up in her neck and face and the light from a lamp she passed caught the bright colour of her hair. It was the same girl that Father James had met running down the road to the beach three days before. He was so surprised that when she walked past him he said nothing, and afterwards his eyes followed her with a strange intent expression as she settled herself on a sofa by the fire. For the minute in which he looked at her, the priest was somewhere else — not in the room nor on the beach road either, but escaped from there into some place where Meriel and the firelight and the substance of her dress were of a single beauty.

'Er, Father,' said Finlay, 'do sit down.' But he was standing in the way of the chairs and sofa. A moment later he asked the priest if he would like another drink. He sat down himself however without waiting for an answer. He began to study his nails attentively, lining them up in a row and examining the fine curve at the tip of each.

The priest sat down beside Anne, holding on to his empty glass because the sliver of ice at the bottom of it cooled his hands. He watched Charles Finlay take out of his pocket a thin stiletto knife — the kind that is sometimes used for opening letters. Finlay turned the knife over and over in his hands and the light shivered up the blade. Father James began to stare at this knife, for its movement both fascinated and repelled him.

'I don't know what's happened to the dinner,' Anne said. 'It's only cold meat.'

Her father turned slightly in his chair and looked at her. He balanced the point of the stiletto on his index finger and caught it again with his other hand. Presently he slipped it back into his pocket and sat drumming his fingers on the arms of the chair.

When the gong rang for dinner the four of them got up from their chairs too quickly, as if the blood had gone to sleep in their veins and needed stirring up again. The old man was wheeled to the door by his son and out across the draughty hall.

The ancestors hung on the dining-room walls in heavy frames. The silver glistened in the candlelight and the napkins were stiffly starched. Sir John sat at one end of the table and his son at the other. They were separated by twelve feet of mahogany, two great candelabra, two silver pheasants and a silver fruit bowl. Charles Finlay went directly to the sideboard and began to carve the cold roast beef.

Sir John leaned towards the priest, stretching his thin neck. 'I'm afraid it will be cold beef,' he said.

'I'm delighted,' said the priest. 'It will make a change from the mutton my housekeeper gives me.'

The old man was no longer listening. He was wiping the corners of his mouth where two patches of spittle had dried and afterwards he sunk his chin onto his chest and stared steadily in front of him. Charles Finlay sat down and his daughters handed round the plates. There were two slices of tender pink beef on each plate, a piece of lettuce, a tomato and a large feathery potato from which the butter ran out in fat gold drops.

Anne Finlay sat down beside the priest. 'Everyone knows Miss Morag is mad,' she said, 'but they can't find anyone to replace her.'

'I must say she doesn't worry me at all,' Father James said carefully. He remembered his anger that morning, and it was like a shameful secret that he shared with his housekeeper. By cutting up his beef into very small pieces and blending them with the rich floury paste of the butter and potato, and by resting each sip of wine against his tongue before he swallowed it, he felt the pleasure of his food rise up like sap in his body.

Charles Finlay suddenly put down his knife and fork and wiped his mouth carefully with a napkin. 'You preached an odd sermon this morning,' he said.

The priest cut up two more pieces of beef and put them into his mouth before replying. A vein throbbed in his neck and he gazed at Finlay in a way which the Laird's son found insolent. 'I'm afraid I don't understand,' he said, 'what you mean by odd.'

'I thought your sermon was awfully good,' Anne said. 'Everyone sat up and listened to you.'

'I don't think', said Finlay ignoring her, 'that your new parishioners understand you. It wasn't the kind of sermon they are accustomed to. Next Sunday if I were you I should try something a little less ambitious.'

'There was nothing ambitious about it,' Father James said quickly. 'I simply wanted them to feel that it matters very much what they do — that the mass should never become a routine exercise which they go through every Sunday and shut off in their minds from the rest of the week. I wanted them to feel that I'm here to give them, well, to help them to have a stronger sense of the importance of it, and the, and the purpose of it, you see,' he said, getting more and more agitated. 'For instance when I say mass every evening at six o'clock, no one comes. Now it's not such a great effort to some of them. I know that most people work all day, but surely even a few of them could spare half an hour — I mean if they understood the importance . . . ' By now, however, he was aware of two things: Charles Finlay had taken his eyes off the priest's face — he was fiddling with the knives and forks around his plate, arranging them precisely in line with the table mat — and Meriel on the other hand was gazing at him with a kind of intensity which also seemed to have nothing to do with what he was saying. Her eyes were an almond shape and they were red brown, the colour of her hair. Light glittered in them from the candles in front of her. The priest was disconcerted and immediately forgot the rest of his argument.

The meal went on in silence and Father James no longer made an effort to break it. Sir John said once, 'I remember this theatre in the Strand — St Martin's I think it was. I went four times to see this play by Noel Coward but which one it was now I can't remember . . . ' At another time while Meriel was pouring cream on to his fruit salad he said ' . . . and there was a restaurant on the corner of Piccadilly where I used to go before the war — Florian's. I saw it one day years afterwards. The sign was still there, just visible. They hadn't bombed it . . . '

After a while he slept with his head bent over the half-empty plate and one hand curled loosely on the table beside him. Once or twice when his head reached a certain angle he woke up and stared round the table as if he had come back from a long journey. The pupils of his eyes were almost white.

When the meal was finished Sir John was wheeled away across the hall. The worn rims of the wheelchair rang out on the bare stone hall and echoed down the back passages until the baize door finally swung shut. Anne went to make some coffee and the priest was left alone with Meriel in the study. She bent down and threw logs on the fire, kneeling with her back to him. Then she swept the grate clean with a small brush and straightened the fire irons. Her hair reached half way down her back. It was finely waved and there were deep bronze lights in it.

The priest sat down and cleared his throat. 'Don't you get lonely here,' he said, 'the whole summer on your own?'

'Oh no,' she said. 'If I could, I should live here all the time — my roots are here,

66

everything that makes me happy — but for you it's different, sent here suddenly when Father Macabe died . . . '

'I have my work. I have a job to do.'

Meriel knelt down before the fire and settled back on her heels. She started on a monologue which had just then come into her head. 'You're lucky to come here while the place is still unspoilt,' she said. 'When I'm in Edinburgh I have nightmares sometimes that Kintillo has changed. I dream,' she went on, 'that the Tourist Board has widened the road across the pass and filled the beaches with caravans, that the whole bay is built over with holiday villas and car parks and refreshment rooms . . . '

'They won't do that for a long time. It would need an enormous amount of money and besides so long as there are landowners like your father . . . '

'But they've already begun. People are putting up bungalows in Camusrury and Camuslang with wrought iron gates and two-tone bells. And this year there were coach tours too from Fort William and Inverness . . . '

Charles Finlay came back into the room. Without saying anything he gave the impression that the room was untidy. He walked restlessly about for a few minutes rearranging ashtrays on the tops of tables, an inch or so one way or another. Finally he sat down and drummed his fingers again on the arms of his chair.

Anne brought in the coffee. 'Nice and strong,' she said, setting down the tray.

He is definitely an army man, Father James thought, looking at Finlay. A great yawn rose up in his chest and pressed against his throat. He clenched his teeth and the yawn subsided. By stretching down to tighten a shoelace he was able to look at his watch: it was only half past nine. For the rest of the time he was there, Meriel scarcely said a word. She pleated up the folds of her black velvet dress in ridges between her fingers and stared dreamily at some point to the left of the fireplace. The priest had the disagreeable feeling that the whole pose was unnatural and that she was somehow forcing him to admire her profile against the light of the fire.

He got up from his chair putting down his empty coffee cup. 'I'm afraid I must go now,' he said. 'I have to get up very early in the morning.'

Finlay considered him for a moment with his strange eyes before getting to his feet. 'I'm afraid you must find it very quiet here,' he said.

'Not at all — I mean that doesn't worry

me.' Charles Finlay had a strange effect on Father James. He found himself tapping the palm of one hand with the other, in the same restless manner.

'No? Good. Well, come again next Sunday. Father Macabe always came on Sunday evenings.' He walked the priest briskly to the door as if it were very late and Father James had outstayed his welcome. His daughters were already collecting up the empty ashtrays and glasses as the young priest turned to say good-bye.

Charles Finlay stood for a while, watching the priest walk away down the drive into the darkness of the trees. The way that he walked alone through the stillness of the park in the coming night, set up a pattern in Finlay's mind of his own strange and bitter isolation: for a while it was he himself, walking in the dusk of some flat and dreary land from which there was no turning back towards the light. At that moment it seemed to him that he was confined to this place until such time as he grew bored to death. So long ago now, that he could remember nothing before it, his elder brother had died. He was drowned at sea in a small boat below the Summer Isles when he was twelve, and Charles only seven or eight. The wrong brother had died — he understood this quite clearly — and he looked after his grief alone. In the upper reaches of the valley he had walked by the source of the river and watched how the water smoothed the stones, and gradually he understood that he was like them — once jagged and full of painful projections but worn smooth at last and beyond hurting, so that he no longer cared for anyone nor they for him.

His daughters had said goodnight and shut the study door behind them. But he stayed by the window staring out into the night and seeing nothing — a yellow square of light from the room behind him threw his shadow out across the drive and the park beyond. He had been twenty-four when he married Mary McGregor. She had sad brown eyes and slightly dirty fingernails but she had a languid softness too, like a warm ripe fruit, and she had many admirers. When Finlay married her he worried immediately how long his extraordinary happiness would last; he thought of it afterwards as the warm season of his life and it lasted until their first child, Anne, was born. Then small changes began to take place which he was quick to notice. Mary became even more careless of the way she looked: her stockings were often laddered and her hands, which she never cared about, were rough from washing clothes and looking after the baby. She insisted on looking after it herself, climbing out of bed in the middle of the night to feed it, and letting no one else touch it. By the time she had her second child her body was thick and flabby and the ripeness of her breasts and hips had spread out into folds the colour of putty. Besides this, she had begun to despise her husband. Her brown eyes mocked him and from somewhere in her weak lazy character she built up an impassive and crushing resistance to him. When he wanted to make love to her, she put down the book she was reading by the bed, submitted without a flicker of interest and picked up the book again as soon as he was done. She was already three months pregnant with their third child before she discussed it with him.

The baby was born too early — just three days before Mary had arranged to go home to Stirling for the birth. He was perfectly made, with long delicate hands and thick dark hair but he only lived for an hour, and two days later his mother died too of a massive haemorrhage. Finlay mourned her death in several ways: he protested against her total absence, the monstrous perfection of his son, and finally against the love that he had lost so many years before. And all these things were like the separate sources of some great flood which was draining steadily out of him and

71

leaving him wasted and empty again.

Mary's sister had taken charge of his daughters and she took them to Edinburgh with her. They lived there until they were old enough to look after themselves and then they spent their summer holidays in Kintillo. At this point, as he stood by the open curtains, a draught coming up from the loose fitting window ledge, Finlay became agitated, going over and over the same ground. For he knew that something was wrong and yet was unable to find a way of putting it right. His daughters were the only two things in his life that he had actually achieved — they were his blood, incredible seeds from his body. And yet they seemed to be nothing to do with him. Anne looked so much like him that at times he seemed to be staring into his own eyes and seeing a vacuum there.

Perhaps he gave them too little, or on the other hand too much: every year he had their bedrooms repainted in the colours they chose; he bought them good horses to ride; he wrote to each of them once a week, sometimes twice. Was this enough? He had no way of knowing — no one to tell him anything. And then there was the new priest, with that fresh timid smile . . . Charles Finlay clenched one hand and rapped it without thinking against the cold window pane. To come into the study after dinner and find them chattering there together, he on the sofa and Meriel at his feet . . . to watch the interest leave their faces just as if he were a stranger walking in. Nevertheless, it was out of the question to put the priest off. It was necessary to submit week after week now, for God knew how long, to these Sunday evenings, to Father James' intolerable enthusiasm and charm.

In spite of his indignation, before going to bed Finlay plumped up the cushions in each chair, placed the fireguard in front of the dead fire and emptied the last cigarette butts into its ashes.

★   ★   ★

That night, while the priest slept, he had a series of brightly-coloured and feverish dreams. In one of them Sir John was walking down the beach with two little girls. The sun was hot and the sea was a dark warm blue. The children were pulling on his arms to make him run, and behind them, stuck fast in the damp sand, Charles Finlay sat in a wheelchair. The sound of his furious shouting was carried away on the wind. One child, when she looked up, had eyes of a light red brown.

5

The next morning when Meriel came down to breakfast, Anne was sitting alone at the table, reading the newspapers. She seemed absorbed by the headlines and neither looked up from the paper nor said good morning. Meriel shrugged. She began to lift the silver covers off the dishes on the sideboard. She lifted them one by one, savouring the smell of the food in each of them. In the first there was porridge, in the second a fine kipper, and in the third there were some fried eggs and bacon. The eggs were cooked just the way she liked them — the whites crisp and the yolks a pale, dense yellow.

'Well,' Anne said suddenly, 'you sat around all evening like a dummy and left me to do all the talking.'

'What?' said Meriel. She lifted the fried eggs tenderly onto a plate and poured herself a cup of coffee.

'I was talking about last night.'

'Ah last night . . . ' Meriel sat down. She gazed out of the window for a minute before beginning her breakfast. It was a perfect summer day. The shadow of the trees across

74

the park had begun to fill out in the morning sun. Beyond them she could just make out the thin line of Raasay, rising from the sea.

'The priest,' Anne was saying, 'had a remarkable kind of beauty.' He reminded her of certain statues, broken-nosed though they were, that she had seen in the Adam Museum in Edinburgh.

Meriel put down her knife and fork and began to laugh. 'No wait,' she said as Anne got up. 'I'm sorry — I didn't mean to laugh at you. To tell you the truth I had forgotten about the priest. I couldn't even tell you what he looks like now.' It was true: until that minute she had scarcely thought about the new priest.

When she was totally self-absorbed, Meriel very often failed to take in what was straight in front of her. Sometimes she looked at certain people second hand: if, for instance, her sister made some comment on them, she would immediately alter her own vague impressions and adapt them to this new image. There was no denying, now when she thought about it, that Father James was a good looking man.

She took a piece of toast, spread it thickly with butter and marmalade and ate it greedily. Anne was gazing at her with her hands on her hips. 'I don't understand you,' she said. 'I don't understand you at all. Anyone who comes to dinner in this place is a big event. Father James is probably the only new face we shall see this side of the autumn and you can't even remember what he looks like.'

Meriel smiled up at her. 'I can't help it,' she said. 'He made no impression on me. He had yellow hair and blue eyes. As for the rest, he was quiet, almost timid. He hardly spoke, did he?' She irritated her sister and she knew it. She began to hum a little tune which had just then come into her head and stretched across the table for the newspaper.

Anne stopped by the door on her way out. 'When you are in this kind of mood,' she said, 'there is no point in talking to you.'

'What kind of mood?'

'If Papa needs me for anything, tell him I shall be out on the drive practising my three point turns.'

When she had gone Meriel poured herself a second cup of coffee and sat down again at the table. She was in an excellent mood. She felt healthy and contented. There had been a time, not long ago, when she was able to count up the number of her conquests on the fingers of one hand. And then in the course of the last summer all this had changed. In the same way that a fully opened flower will suddenly attract bees from all the neighbouring bushes, so Meriel, who to her own way of thinking had scarcely changed, found herself with a great number of new admirers.

She put three lumps of sugar into her coffee and stirred it slowly. In some way however that she could not name, the summer had turned out to be strangely lonely. A cold rain had fallen day after day and the Edinburgh streets were bleak and slippery with a fine black dust from the coalfields in Midlothian. And Meriel, when she thought of the number of men who had kissed her, could only remember them now in connexion with the steady sound of falling rain. One night she had also lost her virginity, and this like other new experiences before it, had turned out to be a bewildering and uncomfortable affair. In the morning her lover had dressed without once looking her in the face, and had left by the basement door without kissing her good-bye. Now when she considered this time as a whole and from a distance, a sudden impatience filled her. She got up from the table quickly without bothering to finish her coffee and went out into the sunlight.

She leant against one of the stone balustrades that led down either side of the great front steps and lifted her face to the warmth of the sun. She began to sing to herself the first song that came into her head. Below her the moving grass, the dark summer trees and even the sheep grazing in the shade, seemed to her like the parts of a single picture especially designed to please her. But presently this impression was entirely ruined by the sound of Anne coming up the drive in the Landrover.

Neither of the two sisters had passed their driving tests and this failure obsessed Anne to the point where she would practise reversing and emergency stops again and again on the drive in front of the house. But while Anne confined herself to the roads around the park, and took care not to ruin the gearbox, Meriel drove fast and carelessly along every road in the peninsula. Last year she had run over a sheep by Camusrury. The sheep had broken a leg and one of the shepherds had been forced to shoot it.

Anne drove past the front steps twice, changing gear smoothly and looking at the same time, for some reason, in the mirror. The third time she went past her, Meriel shouted, 'Hey! How long will you be?' Anne turned the Landrover neatly along the grass verge and came to a stop. She leaned out of the window.

'I wish you wouldn't stand there staring at

me,' she shouted back. 'You put me off.' Meriel came down the steps at a leisurely pace and wandered across the gravel. She had fine long legs and she walked in a lazy graceful way as though she was entirely conscious of them.

'I'm going to see Magnus,' she said. 'When you've finished with the Landrover I'll take it.'

Anne looked at her watch. 'I'll be at least another half hour. You can have it after that. Though what you see in that old drunkard,' she added, 'I shall never know.'

Meriel closed her eyes and smiled. 'Well, he's like a second father to me now,' she said gently.

★   ★   ★

Magnus Laver was sitting on a bench outside his cottage door. It occurred to him to go in and boil up a kettle for some tea and then almost immediately he decided against it. He was warm in the sun and the inside of his cottage was cold and damp. The sun was like a benediction, day after day of it, such weather as he had never seen in the entire ten years he had lived in the Toscaig cottage.

Magnus had once been a London doctor. But about the same time as his teeth had fallen out with a gum infection he had begun to drink too much and to take an interest in philosophy. Over the next few years he continued to practise medicine, but during this time a great gap was springing up between the suffering of his patients and his ability to cure them. The chronically sick still died, the middle aged still complained, and in the middle of their inevitable paths the doctor stood confused, with his bag of medicines and the whisky sometimes in his brain. Throughout this time, he had a certain longing, a dream that he had never actually dreamt, or a picture that he might have seen without remembering where, of a wild clouded coastline, where the sea was a constant line of spray against the rocks and where the mountain peaks were cut off from month to month by a thick mist. It was a place he had never been to in the whole of his life. The dream continued to haunt him however and one day Magnus gave in to it: he decided at last to give up his practice. He put up his small London flat for sale and six months later climbed into his car with his books and luggage and drove north. There was a doctor who regularly sent him Christmas cards — a man he had met one time at a medical conference — and he lived in Ballahuilish. Magnus liked the name of the place, it was on his way and he drove north-west towards it. As he was driving along, he spoke to his wife Mary, who had been dead for several years.

'It's strange,' he said, 'Mary, when you died I hardly touched a drink, and yet, when they took my teeth away, I gave in like a baby after the teat.' Later, he sang to keep his mind off the pubs that were opening up along the road.

When he reached Ballahuilish, his friend, the local doctor, exchanged glances with his wife while Magnus was out of the room, unpacking. 'It's a pity,' these glances indicated, 'that Doctor Laver has let himself go to such an extent.'

'I saw an advertisement for this house in Kintillo,' Magnus said after the evening meal.

'Beautiful,' the doctor agreed, again looking quickly at his wife. 'A little remote, but it will do no harm to go and look at it.'

'I've already leased it,' Magnus said grinning. A moment later he lit a small cigar. 'I was annoyed by my solicitors. I found them too cautious, you see, and when they advised me against it, I decided to lease the place.'

'And you've never even seen it?' This time the local doctor and his wife avoided each other's eyes and stared at the floor between them. Magnus removed his false teeth and tucked them into the breast pocket of his coat. He smiled at his hostess.

'I have trouble with these teeth' he said. 'In general I only wear them to play the clarinet, for otherwise the tone would be affected.'

Mrs Roberts fiddled with a strand of her hair that had escaped from the fine net she wore over it. 'It's been a pleasure meeting you again, Doctor,' she said, 'but if you'll excuse me I'll away to my bed now.'

Doctor Roberts put the fireguard firmly down in front of the fire. 'I'm sure you'll have a fine cottage, Doctor Laver,' he said, 'a fine bargain.'

Magnus took the Ballahuilish ferry next morning across Loch Leven, with a picnic lunch prepared by Mrs Roberts and a bottle of Drambuie that he bought later in Fort William. When he reached the pass of Tornapress, which separated Kintillo from the mainland behind it, Magnus climbed out of his car and looked up at the great black horseshoe ridge with its back to the sun. The road ahead was very narrow — a thin strip that crawled steeply up the mountain shoulder — and round each bend there was the sense that it fell away altogether on the other side. When he climbed back into his car, there was a dark rim around his field of vision from staring into the shadows and his hands trembled on the steering wheel, for he was mortally afraid of heights. On the ferry, the doctor had taken a few mouthfuls of Drambuie straight from the bottle and now it lay beside him on the seat, rolling backwards and forwards with the tilt of each corner. 'If I can just keep my hands off it until I reach the top,' said Magnus, 'we shall be all right.'

His knees began to shake and his breath came in short gasps as though he were running up the heights instead of driving them. Behind him and to the side the pass fell away into a mighty trough and beyond it, strangely, the sun was out. It was shining on Loch Hourn, three thousand feet below.

'God help me,' said Magnus when he reached the top, 'this is far enough away for anyone.' He sighed and uncorked the bottle of Drambuie.

The Toscaig cottage came as a shock to him for it was never included in his dreams. There was a thin sad light on the winter hills and the place looked derelict. A mountain ash grew deep into the walls on one side, and the windows were lopsided and crooked in their frames. 'Don't you think,' Magnus said to the Laird's factor who stood beside him, 'it's a bit ramshackle for the price?' The factor was astonished by the rent himself. He lowered his eyes and fiddled with the keys in his trouser pocket.

'You'd be best to take it however,' he said, 'if you've a mind to live here. The Laird has only three or four cottages to let and the others are already taken. You could go back,' he said, still gazing at the ground, 'to Fort William and try there for somewhere else. I doubt if you'll find so much though.'

'I have already signed the lease,' Magnus said. 'And besides there is the God-forsaken pass — I haven't the stomach to cross it twice in one day.'

'It'll do,' he said at last. He turned and went back down the hill to fetch his luggage.

Magnus had lived in the Toscaig cottage now for over ten years. It had no electricity and no bathroom. The roof leaked intermittently and when it rained he would feel an ache in his knee caps and in the joints of his fingers. He was entrenched there however. He was too old and too weary to go south again.

Suddenly he sat up stiffly and rubbed his eyes. Someone was singing, coming up the hill, out of sight on the steep slope below him. Magnus sighed. He got slowly to his feet. When he saw Meriel Finlay a few yards below him on the path, he took his false teeth from his pocket and put them back into his mouth. Meriel stopped for a moment on the edge of the hill to catch her breath, and the doctor hurried forward to kiss her on both cheeks. He led her towards the bench where he sat her down, first dusting it with a crumpled handkerchief and pulling it out a little from the wall. 'Ah it's good to see you,' he said. 'It's good to see your beautiful face.'

Meriel sat down on the bench beside him and smiled at him. 'Well,' she said presently, 'I like to come up here and listen to your Irish compliments.'

Magnus burst out laughing. 'And you,' he said, patting her hand, 'you get prettier every time I see you.'

Meriel leant back against the cottage wall and shielded her eyes from the light. Below them across the Inner Sound the tip of Raasay sloped down into the sea, and beyond Raasay the mountains of Skye rose clear from the narrow straights between. Their peaks were blue in the morning sun.

'You have the best view, Magnus, in the whole of Kintillo.'

'So I have,' he agreed, 'but I pay for it however. I pay a handsome rent for it.' He had forgotten to eat any breakfast. His stomach felt like an empty pit and from time to time the walls of this pit swelled in and out in gentle spasms.

'I came up to see you before I go,' Meriel was saying. 'Anne and I have been asked to stay for a week with cousins in Portree.'

'Ah . . . '

'I shan't enjoy it though. The cousins feel sorry for us. They wonder what we do all day cooped up here with no parties to go to.'

Magnus studied her. He clicked his teeth together. 'Well,' he said. 'What do you do here? What is there for a girl of your age to do here?'

Meriel shrugged. 'I'm naturally lazy,' she answered. 'I can sit around for hours at a time and do nothing.'

'Nothing at all?' Magnus seemed incredulous.

'Well, I suppose I dream a lot,' for some reason she blushed and avoided looking at the doctor's face. 'I mean, it passes the time.'

Magnus straightened up on the bench. 'It seems peculiar to me,' he started, 'that at your age, when you have almost no memories worth dreaming of, nothing in fact in the way of experience . . . ' In the middle of this sentence his stomach rumbled loudly and Meriel began to laugh.

'You haven't eaten your breakfast yet, have you?'

'It's true, I could do with a cup of tea,' he said apologetically. 'I tell you what — you could put a kettle on now for us both.' While she was inside the cottage the doctor leaned back against the wall and stretched his legs out in front of him. 'What a day,' he said sighing. 'Ah what a day.' The sun was coming down in a slant across the bay and the air was full of a light south wind that carried a smell of bracken and fresh thyme along the shoulder of the hill.

Meriel came back a few minutes later. 'There's no paraffin for the stove,' she said, 'and the fire has gone out too.'

'Ah, has it indeed.' He thought for a moment. 'Then you could bring us some glasses and the whisky that you will find sitting there by the sink — it's near midday after all,' he added.

Presently she came back with the bottle and two glasses and set them down on the ground. 'All the glasses are chipped,' she said smiling at him, 'and the time by my watch is only half past ten.' Magnus giggled guiltily and while he was pouring out the drinks he spilled a little whisky on the grass.

'Aah,' said Meriel. The alcohol burned her throat and brought tears to her eyes. She sipped at it a little at a time and gazed at the colour in the liquid's reflection. 'I like it here,' she said comfortably. 'This is a place where I can talk. I can tell you almost anything.'

They talked for almost two hours. Meriel

leant forward from time to time and picked up a few pebbles from the ground. She would examine them briefly, toss them around between her hands and throw them down again. In the same erratic way, the two of them discussed whatever came into their heads, lightly and without following any one train of thought. Suddenly Meriel looked at her watch and jumped up from the bench. 'Look at the time,' she said. 'It's five to one.'

'Ah relax now,' said Magnus. He was no longer hungry. The whisky had restored his vitality. 'Relax for another five minutes, why don't you? You have the Landrover down there.'

Meriel shook her head. 'No, I really have to go. My father is an army man. He hates unpunctuality.' She kissed him good-bye and stood looking at him for a moment before she went down the path. 'What did you look like,' she said smiling, 'with your real teeth in? I can't imagine you.'

'One day I will find you a photograph of myself as a young man,' he promised her. 'I was really handsome then. My wife Mary chased after me until I married her.'

He walked with her a little way down the path and he waited afterwards until the Landrover had disappeared around a corner of the road. Presently he searched for a tin of sardines in a cupboard by the sink, and he ate them straight from the tin, with a book propped up beside him on the bench outside.

6

In the small villages of the peninsula, the same things happen over and over again. Even the unexpected has a double image to it as if it had occurred some time before in the same way and in the same place. There is a pattern to the week: the mail-boat on Saturday; mass on Sunday; the weekly wash on Monday. So the memory shortens itself and goes from day to day; the pattern is lost among the individual threads and you could be very busy just passing the time in the village shop, or prodding about with a stick on the Forestry Commission land.

In the same way, without noticing it, Father James' ambitions began to shrink to the size of the place he lived in. He gave up hoping for a choir that would do more than sing the carols on Christmas Day. He inquired about an organ for the church but he gave this up too because the roof still needed mending and when the autumn rains came it would leak again over the altar rails.

He decided however to tackle the paint-work inside the rectory. But events had a habit of slipping away and receding into the future. Mactaggart the village painter had recently died. Father James himself had closed the dead man's eyelids and given him extreme unction, and it was Rory Mactaggart the younger who came up to the rectory one morning and moved all the furniture out of the study into the narrow hall. He said, 'Father, would you like a decent job with the blow lamp? Some of this paint's been on the woodwork for over a hundred years.' It was safe to reckon that the diocese would pay for this.

'Yes indeed,' said the priest. 'I think that's an excellent idea.'

'And then there's this new paint against the damp,' Mactaggart said. 'You'd be as well to have that. It's expensive mind, but it's worth it.'

'Yes, well, that sounds all right.'

'Now, you can have a third-rate job done Father — what you would call an economic patching up schedule on the one hand . . . '

'No, I would rather . . . '

' . . . or you can have a first-rate job, on the other hand, which will last you the time you're here . . . '

'Yes I think . . . '

' . . . and well after. This place is in a shocking state as you can see.'

Miss Morag was in the hall behind them.

Father James felt the small hairs at the back of his neck rise up in the draught through the kitchen door. 'Well, I'll leave it to you,' he said, 'to do the first-class job, er . . . Mr Mactaggart.'

'Rory, Father. I'm always Rory to the patrons.'

'Rory then, just as long as you do it as quickly as you can.'

'Certainly, Father, certainly. If Miss Morag could just fix me up with a cup of tea now I'll start on it first thing tomorrow morning.'

'Tomorrow?' the priest said. 'But I thought you were starting right away.'

'Ah well, but I've the van to bring up, the materials and so forth I shall be needing for the duration. And then there's the job I was on when you rang me, Father, down at Thompson's Farm. Naturally I dropped everything to come up here and see you.'

'Well I'm very grateful, but I thought you said on the telephone you could start straight away, right in on it you said.'

Miss Morag was polishing the same strip of bannisters she had been polishing for half an hour now. The priest turned sharply. 'Will you get Mr Mactaggart a cup of tea please?' he said. While she was going out through the door he noticed that his hands were tightly clenched.

'I'll be up first thing in the morning, Father,' Mactaggart said, putting his cap back on his head. 'About nine — will that suit you?'

'Yes that'll be fine,' the priest said.

As Rory was half way through the door to the kitchen he said quickly, 'Perhaps you could come to mass, Rory, first, at half past eight.'

'Er no thank you Father — I'm a Protestant.'

'A Protestant? I'm sorry — I thought I saw your name on the Parish register.'

'Er well — I'm a Protestant convert you see. About nine tomorrow then — I'll make a grand job of it.'

Rory Mactaggart turned up the next day but his blowlamp was temperamental and Father James understood that he would have to do without his study for some time and would go on grazing his shins on the furniture in the narrow hall practically every time he went up and down the stairs.

One midday, the priest was sitting outside the rectory in the long grass, reading his breviary. Once this grass had been a lawn but now it was tangled and spotted with dark patches of clover and sea flowers that resisted the salt west wind, and it was hemmed in by a tumbled wall from which about a quarter of the stones had fallen down on either side. Now the wall stood rickety and stump-toothed and the grass grew up the sides almost to the top of it. The grass was cool and sweet smelling of shrivelled pinks and wild thyme and lemon balm. He crushed the lemon balm between his fingers because this scent reminded him of a summer long ago, when lying in a field looking up through the thick grass stems he saw a whole new country there, two inches from the ground.

'I had an early meal,' said Rory Mactaggart. He leaned through the window with the unlit blowlamp in one hand. He held the blowlamp like a tankard cradled against his chest. The priest put down his breviary and straightened up on one elbow in the grass. 'It's grand weather we're having,' said Mactaggart.

The priest agreed. The shadows of the sycamores shifted up and down, and the grass moved a little in a lift of wind.

'I hear you're thinking of having a jumble sale, Father.'

The priest sat upright. 'I was only discussing it an hour ago in the village shop,' he said. 'I'm amazed . . . '

'Things travel,' Mactaggart said. 'You might say the very stones are listening in.'

'It's only an idea so far,' the priest said,

'and it won't make much money this year or even next. But the main point is not the money we'll get out of it . . . ' He turned and looked up towards the point where Rory Mactaggart was leaning on the window sill. 'It's the chance to get the parish together, to get them working on something outside themselves, all those people who have nothing to do, who are isolated or lonely or neglected in some way . . . '

Mactaggart scratched one ear with the handle of the blow-lamp. 'Excuse me, Father,' he said, 'but you're not talking about anybody I know. Everyone has something to do even if it's just sitting on the door stoop smoking a pipe.'

'But how many of you really work? I mean a good day's work with wages in your pockets to spend.'

'Well,' Mactaggart said, 'I should say about half the population. So long as the Laird is alive and his son after him.'

'Only half. Well then, you see? It's ridiculous. At least I could find work for some of you — not permanent perhaps — but there are plenty of things to be done that badly need doing . . . '

'Excuse me, Father, but what things?'

'Well, according to Father Lanni . . . '

'With respect to your profession, Father,

he's a fool. He's a fool who has lived here for decades and understands nothing about the place at all. He says, 'Get the Forestry Commission up here. Plant fir trees — forests of firs.' Would you like to see these hills covered in dark green squares and triangles? Regular regiments of them? And who would get the real benefit? Not us, not the people who live here. He says, 'Get the fishing industry going.' He knows nothing about it. Does he know, for instance that the lobster fishers are going as far south as Northumberland to find work? That they tip the fish back into the sea for lack of transport? That right this year they've closed the railway to Inverness from the Kyle and they're even talking now of closing the tracks to Mallaig, the biggest fishing port on this part of the coast? He knows nothing.'

'And yet,' the priest said, getting to his feet and sitting down again propped on the garden wall, 'and yet he is right about one thing. With the present rate of people leaving this coast, in twenty years' time there will be no one living here. Unless something is done to hold them back, in fifty years the roads will go to ruin and this area will be uninhabitable. I've wanted to come here for a long time. I've read all I could find about the place — your history, your economy, your traditions. Unless you fight for them now and quickly they'll be gone during your lifetime.'

'That's been said from a long way back,' Mactaggart said mildly. He put the blowlamp down on the window-sill and gazed out across the bay. 'It was said at the Rising of the '45. It was said in the Year of the Sheep and about every year since.'

'That doesn't mean it won't finally happen.'

Mactaggart shrugged. 'Why did you want to come up here, Father?'

Suddenly the priest flushed. 'I don't think I could answer that in a way you would understand. And besides I don't see what that has to do with anything we were saying.' He stopped to brush the grass seed from his black cloth suit. Across the beach the children let out of school ran zig-zag up and down the sand throwing stones at the seagulls and the seagulls were screaming from the water's edge as if they had actually been hit.

'Then if I had to guess,' the painter said, 'I'd say suppose you came to get away — to get away from all those troubles in the south, from the dirty air to this air that's sweet and clean, from all that chasing after money to this place where there's not much money and nothing to spend it on. Suppose you came here because . . .'

'I didn't come here to get away. I came here to do something.'

'Suppose you came here because we've a different kind of trouble here — something a man could get hold of and change. Maybe you can't change the other because it's going too fast. One man can't do much in a big city — just a little here and there. But in this place he would have a chance to breathe and to make something of himself and the place he lived in. No offence meant, Father, but there are plenty others of you out there along this coast.'

'Others of me?' The priest was getting restless. His lunch was late. An odd politeness kept him there when he should have gone back into the house.

'Don't you see, Father?' Mactaggart said patiently. 'So long as there's others of you longing for the empty land, and there's plenty of them — so long as there's others coming here to get away from the big cities and so long as there's some of us content to live here too the way we've always done, then the Highlands will survive. And that', he said, 'will be any ways until I die.'

Miss Morag was at the rectory door, pulling and kicking at the bottom where it had dropped on its hinges with the damp.

'I'm coming,' the priest shouted. Rory

Mactaggart put his head back through the window and lit the blowlamp.

'Your dinner's on the table,' Miss Morag said. She had finally opened the door and was standing there shielding her face from the brilliant sun.

As the priest walked into the dining room Mactaggart appeared again, this time round the study door. 'Excuse me, Father,' he said, 'but about the jumble sale — no sense in hurrying things.' Before the priest had his mouth open to reply, Mactaggart's head had disappeared again around the door and he began to sing above the tearing of the blowlamp.

Something happened in the following week that put the jumble sale entirely out of Father James' mind. He came back very late from Dornie on the Sunday night, and the following morning he went into the post office to collect his groceries. 'Did you not hear, Father?' the postmistress said in her calm voice. 'Rory Mactaggart broke three ribs and both his legs last Saturday after the football match in Glasgow. He fell from a window thirty feet. It's a miracle he's still alive.'

The priest was astonished. 'What a terrible thing,' he said. 'How did it happen?'

'Well, he had this fight in a bar on

Sauchiehall Street — a fight with a rival football fan. His ear was sliced off by a bottle, and seeing how much he had drunk, he felt no pain. Well,' she went on, 'when he saw the kind of hospital they had taken him to, poor Rory forgot about the stairs and took a dive from the first floor window to get out of it again . . . '

'I'm really sorry to hear that. What a terrible thing,' he said again.

'And then the ear,' she added, 'I think they found it afterwards in the road. Is there anything else you'll be needing then, Father?'

As the priest drove home his astonishment grew. Rory was a gentle man not connected in his mind with football matches and violent accidents nor indeed with the big cities which he seemed to despise. These events appeared to have happened to a different man, one he had never met.

When he reached the rectory he put the heavy box of groceries down upon the kitchen table. Miss Morag was standing as she always did pressed into the darkest shadows in a corner of the room. 'There's a young lady to see you.'

'A young lady? Who?'

'Miss Meriel. She's in the church. She wants confession.'

'Oh,' said the priest. He turned away and

looked out of the window as though he expected to see her standing there inside the vestry door. He could just make out the church through the dark heavy leaves of the sycamore trees. The idea of hearing Meriel Finlay's confession was somehow disagreeable to him. 'I won't be long,' he said. 'I'll have my lunch at the usual time.'

Inside the vestry there was no sound at all — nothing, in fact, to indicate that Meriel Finlay was there behind the screen. The air in the small room was stifling and the pine chair creaked as he sat down in it.

Meriel cleared her throat. 'It's three weeks since my last confession,' she began.

Father James gazed out of the vestry window. The sky was a single square of plain blue and half another. The sun was a long way above him on the grey slate roof. Meriel went through her minor faults and the priest said nothing. He waited to see what had brought her up the hill on such a beautiful week-day morning. She told him at last, that there was nothing to do in Kintillo. The weather was hot and she would sit sometimes on the beach alone and long for someone to make love to her. And again in bed at night the same thoughts would go on tormenting her until she was sick of them and could not sleep . . . At times she spoke so softly that the priest had to lean against the screen to hear her at all.

'How old are you?' he asked her presently.

'Nineteen.'

'Well then, at your age these thoughts are perfectly normal. It's only when they become an obsession or even a habit that there is anything wrong in them.'

'But I am obsessed . . . '

At this point he was suddenly incredulous. He felt certain, without knowing why, that her entire confession was false. 'Are you obsessed?' he asked gently.

There was no answer from behind the screen. Father James sighed. He tilted the chair slightly backwards and stretched his legs, for they had been pressed against the wall in one position. 'I don't ask you to suppress these thoughts entirely,' he said in a flat monotone. 'I would like you however to try and control them a little, And, if it's possible, to spend less time on your own. It is wrong for girl of your age to be alone too much.'

In general, the confessions he was hearing would sift through his mind without leaving a single impression. Very often they were simply a list repeated from one confession to the next so that, like a doctor listening again and again to the same complaints, he would give out the same penances and repeat the same small homilies. Sometimes he was moved by pity or even sympathy and at other times, however, he would feel a sudden sharp impatience. There was, for instance, a small group of people — mostly frustrated married women or young girls — who would deliberately set out to shock him. They would describe their married lives to him in great detail, leaving nothing out; or they would lean against the screen and try to provoke him into discussions on sex and morality. It had occurred to him while he was listening to Meriel Finlay that she might be one of these. Then almost immediately he was ashamed of himself.

He asked her if she had anything else to confess. She told him there was nothing — nothing of any importance.

'Then make a good act of contrition and pray to God to give you peace of mind.'

There was a wasp trapped against the vestry window. The window was open — in fact it was warped and would not shut — but the wasp repeatedly climbed up the bottom pane as far as the wooden surround, then it would fall to the ledge and start out again on the same journey a second later. This noise distracted the priest and interfered with the words of absolution. 'In the name of the

Father,' he said, raising his voice, 'and of the Son and of the Holy Ghost.'

'Amen.'

'Go in peace,' he said as Meriel got up to leave, 'and pray for me.'

When he came out of the church she was standing awkwardly in the middle of the cinder path waiting for him. She wore a grey pleated skirt, dark nylon stockings and a black blazer, and Father James was even more irritated, seeing that she had dressed up specially for the occasion.

'I'm sorry,' she said, 'my father told me to tell you, if I saw you again soon, that perhaps you could come to dinner every other Sunday. My grandfather's getting too old now, you see . . . '

He nodded. 'Tell him I'll come once a month instead — perhaps that's better. Tell him I'll ring him.'

'All right I'll tell him that.' She started off down the cinder path at once. The priest turned away and went back through the rectory gate. As he shut it behind him, he couldn't avoid seeing, from a distance, the deep copper red of Meriel's hair as she went down the road. She was running again, like a child let out of school.

7

Meriel could no more stop herself from running down that hill than the birds on the beach below her could stop from rising, singly or in thick flocks, circling for a time in the warmth of the sun, and settling again in the same patches of sand as before. And so long as she was running, she had no worries at all, felt nothing but the wind lifting her hair and the heat of the midday sun in her face.

But when she reached the foot of the hill she was out of breath and sat down for a while on the bridge. This bridge crossed the mouth of the Kintillo river. On one side the water was clear and ran freely, but on the other, it sank almost without a trace into the silt of the bay. Meriel leant against the bridge and looked down into the water, and then abruptly, as though she had seen her own reflection there, she got up and began to walk on along the road.

She was mortally ashamed of herself. No one in the whole of Kintillo had ever seen her in a skirt; and even worse than this she was parading along the beach at midday in high-heeled shoes and dark stockings. She turned quickly through the lodge gates into the shade of the north drive. Here she was hidden from the park by a thick belt of trees and from the open valley by the side woods. The side woods were cold and secretive. As a child it had seemed to her that a person might die there and that his body would overgrow with creepers and one day resemble nothing but a fallen log to anyone passing by. Just then however she found the darkness comforting and presently she slowed down and began to walk again in her usual slouching way. She considered the morning behind her with a mixture of shame and fear.

That morning, as usual she had dressed hurriedly and without interest, picking up a pair of jeans from the floor where she had thrown them down the night before. Through the window as she zipped them up she could see her sister on a bay mare, trotting down the drive towards the road. Anne wore smart grey breeches and her hair was tied in a bun. As she rose up and down to the movement of the trot, the seat of her breeches caught the light, and presently Meriel watching her from the window began to imitate her, sticking out her bottom and rising up and down in the same precise and finicky manner. In the middle of this charade however she stopped what she was doing and stood with her arms hanging loose by her sides. For she had seen her own reflection in the dressing table mirror. She was still naked to the waist and in the strong light from the window her body looked magnificent. The flesh of her arms and neck was white and smooth and beneath her breasts there were two deep shadows the shape of crescent moons. She stood there for a moment longer, turning slightly from one side to another so that the light caught her body from different angles and then she sat down to brush her hair.

From time to time in the past week Meriel had allowed her thoughts to rest lightly on the priest. She had made up a number of daydreams about him and these at first were almost harmless. But now while she sat half naked on the dressing stool she smiled at her reflection in the mirror. This smile was sly and secretive, for an amazing scene had just come into her head. There were only two figures in this scene and one of them was Father James. He was standing at the rectory door in the morning sun and before him wearing a light fawn raincoat and flimsy sandals stood Meriel Louisa Finlay . . .

'Come in,' the priest was saying. He stood a little back from the door. 'What can I do for you?' Meriel walked ahead of him into the small study. Her eyes were cast down and she stood in the middle of the room with her hands clasped neatly in front of her. 'I'm afraid it's a little stuffy in here.' Father James made an effort to open the window but the runners were loose and almost immediately it closed again. 'Do sit down, won't you,' he said turning round, 'and take off your things.'

'Thank you father.' Obediently his guest began to take off her coat. With one hand she undid the buttons and with the other she modestly held the edges shut. When the last button was undone, she stepped out of it neatly and allowed it to fall to the floor. Beneath the raincoat Meriel had nothing on at all . . .

At this point in her daydream Meriel covered her mouth with her hands and started to laugh. And when she looked in the mirror her eyes were shining brilliantly. 'One day,' she said softly to herself aloud, 'I will do it.'

She picked up the hairbrush again and tilted her hair backwards so that the whole tender weight of it fell down her back almost to the waist. Just as she longed to go up the hill dressed in such a way she could see at once that she would do nothing of the kind. The rest of this little scene was not clear to her at all and it was certain, besides, to turn out badly.

Presently another plan began to form in her mind — one which was altogether different and almost harmless. She settled herself more comfortably on the stool and began to make up her eyes. She spread two wings of shadow across each lid and applied a thick coat of mascara to the upper and lower lashes. Presently she searched out, among the muddle in her drawers, her last good pair of stockings, her cleanest shirt and a smart pleated skirt. In the same excellent spirits she walked up the road to the rectory and knocked on the door, and while she stood there waiting for the priest, she briefly revised the confession she had just made up.

There were two things wrong with her plan, however, which she had not foreseen. From the beginning of her confession Meriel had felt a sense of shame; and this feeling reached a point where she longed to get up and leave again. And later, while she stood talking with the priest on the cinder path outside, something totally unexpected and painful had taken place. For Meriel, looking up for a minute into the priest's face had seen in his eyes her own reflection, and this reflection was immediately cheap and repulsive to her.

She had now walked the entire length of

the north drive without noticing her sur-
roundings. Within a hundred yards of the
house the thick trees fell away to either side of
it and the broad light of the midday sun cut
into the edges of the woods. The house
looked white and shrunken in the glare and
the open park was deserted.

Meriel calculated that it would take her
about half a minute to reach the side door
and another to get to the safety of her room.
With her shoes in one hand she ran in her
stockinged feet across the gravel and she
reached the side door just as the gun dogs
had begun to bark in the stable yard. The
stone back stairs were cold underfoot and she
stumbled in the sudden darkness. No sound
came up the stair well from the kitchen and
the first floor landings were empty. Most of
the bedrooms had been cleaned and the
windows and doors left open so that a fresh
cool draught ran through the upper hall and
along the airless passages.

Meriel shut her bedroom door and leaned
against it resting. She took off the pleated
skirt and left it lying on the floor. She threw
down the blazer in the same way and then she
lit a cigarette and surveyed the room. There
were piles of unfolded clothes on the chair
and on the floor around her bed. On her
dressing-table there were jars without tops to

them and an empty Kleenex box stuffed with rubbish. From time to time Meriel would sort out the bottles and jars and hang up the clothes in the cupboard again. But generally these fits of tidiness would begin to seem pointless after a short while and the mess would then build up again gradually and without being noticed.

That morning, however, the whole room disgusted her and she started to work on it with a sudden impatience. She cleared the floor, the dressing table and even the insides of the drawers. And by the time the gong rang for lunch she was hot from the unaccustomed work and quite satisfied with the general effect. The bed was neatly made and the cover drawn over it. Fresh air had lifted the smell of cigarettes from the room and the full south sun shone at an angle across the empty floor.

But in the evening of that same day, for no reason at all, a bewildering sadness filled her. For a long while she sat looking out of the window, gazing at nothing, and later she wrote in the fly leaf of a book she was reading, 'I am now nineteen and yet nothing of any importance has ever happened to me.'

8

The heatwave was coming to an end. Far to the west the first clouds had already appeared, coming down across the shoulders of the Cuillins. They gathered slowly in a straight line across the peaks, waiting for a wind to drive them in towards the mainland. On the last evening of July, about eight o'clock, Father James took a walk up the valley to the peat loch Doonican, on the disused road which was overgrown and dusty. High summer poppies and harebells that the sea winds shrivel, grew there in thick patches and in the valley fields along the river. The trees were sharply separated from one another and almost flat against the sky beyond. Nothing moved in the heavy copper light and there was the kind of stillness that comes before a sudden change as if the climate took leave of one season in a certain lull, before beginning the next.

The priest felt exhausted and quite relaxed. He was so tired that his brain had lost its natural process of selection. He noticed odd pieces of rubbish in the road, once a rusty tin and later on an old shoe, as though these objects were suddenly important to him. And when a brightly coloured pebble caught his eye he stopped for a moment to pick it up, thinking he had dropped something. Yet when he finally noticed Meriel Finlay, she was not more than ten feet away from him, sitting on a five-barred gate. Shock, like a shutter, closed in his brain. He stood without moving in the middle of the road and stared at her.

Meriel had watched him coming down the road. The dust flew up over his shoes and small pebbles rattled towards the verge from under his feet. These were the only sounds in the silence of the coming storm. Sitting quietly on the gate, she had hoped he might pass her without looking up. But now the priest was staring at her as though he had walked into a trap. 'I was just sitting here,' she said. 'I mean — I was just going.'

Father James sighed. He was stupefied by the heat and by his own surprise. Meriel was sitting on the gate with her skirt hitched up around her thighs. From where he stood he could see the entire length of her legs. The heat was now inside him, a suffocating heat which centred in his stomach and loins. He tried to disconnect himself from her, thinking of things at random, but his mind refused to focus on anything. The effort seemed too great and he knew that sooner or later, he would look at her legs again. He cleared his throat. 'I'm sorry, I didn't hear you. Did you say you were going?'

When she answered him he watched her mouth moving as though no sound came out of it and yet her body seemed quite close to him. He could see clearly the freckles on her upper arms and the dust on her bare feet; and while she climbed down off the gate he shut his eyes and gave in again to the strange panic of his body, in which the blood seemed to move more swiftly and to flood into the roots of every nerve.

Meriel came up and stared at him. When he opened his eyes again she stood directly in front of him peering anxiously into his face. 'Are you all right?' she asked. 'You look very pale.'

'Yes, I'm fine thank you. It was just the heat. I'm all right now.'

'You look tired. Come and sit down — there, where it's cool.'

'No I — no thank you. I felt a little strange. Now it's gone. I must be going — it's getting dark.'

Meriel was puzzled. 'It won't be dark for another four hours.'

'No . . . nor it will. I was forgetting.'

With an effort he walked away from her and leaned against the gate. If she was behind

114

him or in front of him it made no difference. He was aware of her and of nothing else. And although he gazed out across the field a vivid and detailed picture now tormented him. He could see her naked body as clearly as though he touched it: her breasts which were round and full, the nipples pale and the veins surrounding them blue and fine beneath the skin. And her legs, of which he had just had such an excellent view, now stretched in a long slender line to the foot of his bed.

Meriel, meanwhile, was leaning on the gate beside him making polite conversation in the same nervous way that a hostess would chat to an awkward guest. ' . . . and when I look over there,' she was saying, 'towards the south, it reminds me of Edinburgh and of all the things I hate . . . Imagine the typing course I'm doing for instance . . . ' She paused for a minute and the priest sensed that she was looking at him. He said nothing, however, and continued to stare in a blank way at the field.

He had spent three hours driving to Kyle of Lochalsh hospital and three hours driving back again. He had spent two hours in the hospital wards, saying mass behind screens with the smell of ether in his nostrils and the sight of pain for which he could do nothing. And now, when he was vulnerable, for want of the strength to get away, he leant on the gate beside her and listened to the sound of her voice without hearing a word she said.

If I don't leave at once, he thought, I shall be certain to touch her, first perhaps just her elbow and then . . . and how had it happened? How did they come to be standing so close together, almost touching? In such a place? Meriel was still talking, breaking off now and then to see if he was listening. 'How young she is for her age,' he thought, 'she is still a child.' And then immediately he knew that this was not the case, for this same child had the sweet sly instincts of a grown woman And besides this, her body was filled with a powerful sexuality, so that any man standing so close to her would probably feel the same physical confusion . . . All at once he was so exhausted that he felt a kind of anguish, an urge to clench his fists and cry out to be left alone.

Being careful not to look at her he said at last, 'You ought to go now. Your father will be wondering where you are.'

She looked at him anxiously again. 'You still look pale. Are you sure you will be all right? I'll go now if you want me to. I only stayed . . . '

'No you go. I'll be all right. It was just the heat.'

But Meriel still hesitated for some reason as though deciding whether or not to shake him by the hand and it was the priest, at last, who turned and started to walk away from her down the road.

A little way along the dusty track he turned briefly to wave good-bye. She was perched again on the top of the gate with her bare feet hooked under one of the bars. But the air of the coming storm seemed to thicken and grow solid around her so that even from a short distance he could no longer see her clearly.

The priest went on with his walk, but his eyes were fixed on the road and it was some time before he noticed that he was going in the wrong direction. Only half an hour earlier he had left the rectory in order to escape for a while from its gloomy atmosphere and now within minutes that pretty Georgian house which looked so inviting from the outside world would enclose him again in the same stifling grip as before.

It was impossible now to turn round and go on with his walk for Meriel Finlay was somewhere close behind him in the valley: and if he stopped for a moment he would hear her footsteps on the empty road. The priest blamed Meriel. He blamed her bitterly for his present discontent. The more he tried to analyse the situations in which they had met, the more convinced he became that she had set out to seduce him. His first impressions of her false dreaminess and of her posing were stronger now; and he added to these the strange coincidence of their meeting in the road and even that of her confession, as parts of a single plan, perhaps begun in boredom, to infuriate and unbalance him.

During the past few weeks a subtle erosion had taken place in his state of mind: questions arose which he had never considered asking himself before, and now he longed also for the most ordinary things that he had learned to do without. He started to imagine himself, for instance, sitting in the window of a coffee bar in Oxford Street, looking affectionately through the glass at those very crowds which before he had found so unremarkable; or even queuing for a bus and climbing up the narrow steps to the top, simply for the pleasure of lighting a cigarette. It was the mediocrity of life that he missed so unexpectedly. Good food, good company — the loss of such luxuries is so tremendous that there is even a certain gaiety in giving them up. Noise, however, the useless noise of crowds, and even their ugliness, were things that he now needed and felt suddenly deprived of.

There was someone in whom he longed to confide. He had a cousin, an administrator in the diocese of Salford, and whenever he wanted advice, or simply a friend to turn to, Father James would write to him. Now, when he thought of this, he quickened his pace in the road and for the first time that evening, he looked up and noticed the storm which was coming in across the sound. In a little while the first rain would fall and the drought would come to an end.

★　★　★

When Father James went out in the evenings, Morag watched him from the rectory windows until he was out of sight. There was scarcely a time in her working day when she didn't know of his whereabouts; she had him on a string, loose-played and slack, but she knew whether he went by foot or took his car and she waited until he came back again, no matter what time of night. She watched him at ease in the rooms which did not belong to him. He slept in the dead priest's bed, and got up in the church to give sermons on subjects which Father Macabe had never touched upon.

He ill-treated her also in a number of ways.

He was silent when she came into a room, he would sit with a book propped up in front of him when she served his food and later he would leave the meal half eaten on the plate. For each of these insults Morag had found an answer. At one time she put drops of water into the salt and shoved it on to the table in hard lumps. 'I don't know what's with it,' she said. 'It's nivver done that before.' The priest had merely smiled.

At another time, while she was cleaning his shoes she put a small stone beneath the inner sole of one of them and there was a satisfied look on her face that morning as she swept out the house and prepared his midday meal.

Although the priest scarcely seemed to notice her nor to take account of her behaviour, Morag had changed in subtle ways. Now she walked about the house with an unaccustomed spring in her shambling walk and sometimes she would rest in her work and gaze at the ground in front of her with a queer smile as though there had just then come into her head a strange and savage joke.

Sometimes when her work was finished and the priest was not at home, she would go out for a while and take a little fresh air. On such evenings when the sun still rested above the high tips of the Cuillins, and when the valley below her was drowsy and settled, Morag took from the coal shed an old deck chair, which a former priest had bought in Inverness. She would drag it from the shade of the house and up the cinder path towards the churchyard. The cemetery lay under the brow of the hill and the late sun came down at a slant across it so that the shadow of each grave was long and thin, and pointed east towards the hills. It took her a certain time to get the deck chair to the foot of the cemetery for it clattered noisily over the uneven ground and got caught among the gravestones. Down against the slope, she would lay the deck chair out, fuss a little with the angle of the seat, and settle at last to the widest view in the bay of Kintillo. On those nights when the bleating of a sheep on the far mountain slopes sounded clear and close at hand, Morag sat alert in her chair and was sensitive to the slightest movement in the valley below her.

Father James, that evening, was still walking slowly along the road from Loch Doonican when she first noticed him. She had time without hurrying to fold the deck chair up against the wall. When that was done she stood harmlessly by the graveyard wall, one eye gazing at nothing and the other fixed on Father James.

Perhaps because her heart began to beat at

a wild irregular rate, Morag had already absorbed the shock of what she saw next before it took place. Less than a hundred yards behind the priest, walking in her indolent way and scarcely lifting her feet off the ground, came Meriel Finlay — back down the same road that he had taken — and though she crossed the river and took a side gate into the park, Morag could see that she stopped for a minute in the road and looked up towards the rectory. And into this look she read so much guilt that Morag threw back her head and laughed aloud by the cemetery wall.

9

'I'm afraid my daughters are not here,' Finlay said, handing the priest a glass of sherry. 'They have gone to stay with cousins in Portree.' He glanced sharply for a moment at Father James to see if he could detect a look of disappointment in his face. The priest had taken the news quite calmly, however, and even seemed relieved. He merely smiled and sipped at a little of his sherry.

'It was a terrible storm we had the other night,' he said after a pause. 'Several slates fell off the rectory roof.'

'Terrible,' Finlay agreed. He looked at his watch. 'If you'll excuse me for a minute I must fetch my father from his room. And then I think we might go directly into dinner. Since the food is cold,' he added.

The priest drained his glass in a hurry and shuddered slightly for this particular brand of sherry left a sweet and cloying taste in his mouth. The claret they drank with the meal, however, was excellent.

'Chateau Batailley 52,' Sir John said loudly, turning the bottle towards him and reading out the label. 'It should have been decanted. I remember,' the old man went on, 'the last time we had a bottle of this. It was in April when Magnus Laver came to dinner.'

Charles Finlay put down his soup spoon in the plate. He waited for this piece of foolishness to sink into the sudden silence. 'Doctor Laver,' he said firmly, 'has not dined here for at least eight years.'

'Well I still remember it all the same,' the old man repeated stubbornly, 'and this is exactly what we drank. We had some pheasant and several bottles of the Batailley.'

'I'm sorry to contradict you father, but I think you've confused that evening with another. This wine would have been too young to drink at the time when Laver was here. He has not been inside the house for the past eight years and on that occasion he was so drunk that he fell against the Sheraton desk in the drawing-room and damaged it so badly we were unable to get it mended.'

The old man was no longer listening. A bead of barley from the soup they were eating had lodged between two of his false teeth. With great patience he sucked and ferreted at this piece of barley until he had anchored it with his tongue and swallowed it.

The priest helped his host to clear away the soup plates, and presently they sat down again to some cold ham with Cumberland sauce, mashed potatoes and Brussels sprouts. Father James was finding the evening motionless and flat, like something he was going through in his memory afterwards. When he had first heard that Finlay's daughters were away he had felt nothing but a great sense of relief. And then almost immediately in the wake of this he felt cheated. In the same way that a well-trained athlete would look forward to his next meeting with an opponent by whom he had been badly beaten, so the priest had prepared himself in advance for an evening with Meriel Finlay. He had been quite certain moreover, of the way she would look, in the same black dress she had worn before, and by the same turns chattering and oddly silent, while he himself remained aloof and vague. With an effort he pulled himself together and was just about to speak when Charles Finlay leant towards him and asked him if he had met the doctor yet.

'So far I haven't,' he answered. 'I should like to get to know him though. The people in the village talk so much about him, don't they?'

Charles Finlay cut up the meat on his plate before replying. He speared each square with his fork and added the same amount of potato and Brussels sprouts. Finally he doused the whole forkful in Cumberland sauce before putting it into his mouth. 'I think I should warn you about the doctor,' he said and stopped. He was going to say, 'The doctor is a drunkard. It will do your reputation no good to be seen with him.' Then it occurred to him that some slight scandal involving the new young priest might be among the first small steps towards the priest's departure. Almost stealthily an idea had already formed at the back of his mind to be rid of him. Finlay wasn't used to dealing squarely with ideas of this sort and he was more inclined to chip away at them gingerly, so as not to disturb his central self-esteem.

During the meal he fiddled with the knives and forks around his plate, as though the conversation was so boring that he could scarcely control his hands. In reality, he was quite unconscious of them. He was staring, without seeming to do so, at the priest. The first evening he had met Father James — (already a month ago but hate made him more familiar) — he had looked carefully into the priest's face for some sign of warmth but Father James had avoided this look as if it were disagreeable to him, and averted his eyes. Charles Finlay took this as a total rejection, yet another instance of his own isolation, and during the dinner that followed — every detail of which, again by reason of his loathing, he still remembered — he had searched for and despised all the tricks of the young priest's charm. He himself was incapable of saying things he did not mean, nor of laughing at jokes he did not find funny. Charm was a luxury he had been born without: it was as much of a mystery to him as any other talent he did not possess. 'It's just as well my daughters are away,' he thought. 'It's exactly this kind of empty charm that young girls find attractive.'

While he stared at Father James' profile in the candlelight a sudden idea struck him which was so obscene it made him feel giddy. He saw distinctly for a moment in front of him, the spectacle of Father James making love to his daughter Anne, and the naked flesh of their buttocks and legs shone in the same candlelight he was now gazing dimly towards. Such a rage overwhelmed him that it was almost voluptuous. He closed his eyes and withdrew his hands from the table, clenching them in his lap.

At the other end of the table Sir John slept soundly. Saliva had formed a bubble in his open mouth and this bubble went in and out with his breathing. From time to time, Charles Finlay looked at him and frowned slightly but the meal continued and the conversation went on in the same sporadic way as before. The boredom of the whole evening now weighed on the priest to such an extent that he too was becoming drowsy, and when he fixed his eye on one of the Georgian candlesticks in front of him its silver stem began to twist about and swell oddly in the light. He had just stifled another urge to yawn when Charles Finlay rose at last to his feet.

'I'm afraid I have to take my father to bed now,' he said. 'When we are dining alone he is usually taken to his room a little earlier.'

Father James also rose from the table, a trifle too eagerly.

'Perhaps I should go then,' he offered. 'You've been very kind to ask me. It was an excellent dinner.' He looked briefly at the wine, for there was a good half bottle which remained unfinished on the table. He smiled at his host, however, and stretched out his hand to say good-bye.

Finlay shook hands with him quickly and without looking directly into his face. And a few moments later as he was showing Father James to the door, he directed such a look of loathing at his back that he wondered the young priest did not stumble under the weight of it. But Father James noticed nothing and went on down the steps into the drive. When he turned a second later to say good-bye, the great front door was already closing behind him.

10

The priest said mass a little earlier on Saturdays. He went down to the mail-boat at nine in the morning to pick up his letters, the provisions for the church and any parcels — sometimes books, sometimes food — sent by his family and friends. He met Magnus Laver by the boat while he was waiting for the mail bags to come out of the hold. The boat was a morning's attraction, a magnet which drew most of the villagers out of their cottages towards the pier, where they stood about in idle groups. There was a noise of chains and a strong smell of fish. The sea gulls flew in and out of the boat's rigging, screaming and lunging at the decks.

Doctor Laver leant forward and shouted something in the priest's ear. When Father James turned round he was shocked for a minute to see that the old man had no teeth. 'Will you have a drink with me, Father, in the post office,' Magnus shouted, 'that is, if you don't object?'

'Not at all,' the priest shouted back. 'I'm cold. It will do me good.'

At that moment he glanced towards the

boat. Meriel Finlay was getting off it, helped by a sailor down the gangplank. She wore a white Arran sweater and a scarf around her dark red hair. She looked once towards the priest and turned away. Father James felt that he stood alone, with his black cassock flapping in the wind, as conspicuous as a beacon on the top of a hill, and that every face in the parish had turned to stare in the silence not at Meriel but at him. This feeling lasted only a moment, but when he turned to follow Magnus into the post office, he was cold and his eyes smarted suddenly from the wind and from the grit on the pier.

Inside the post office, there were too many people crammed into the small space and the noise was even louder, magnified by the low ceilings and the crowded walls.

Jeanie took the two men through the flap of the counter into her little sitting room. 'Pay no attention to what you hear about Doctor Laver,' she said softly to the priest. 'He's a good man like yourself, Father.'

Magnus took a bottle and two glasses from a cupboard on the wall. 'Now you have great honesty, Jeanie.' He held the bottle to the light. 'Not a single drop has been touched,' he said, grinning at her.

Jeanie blushed. 'I'll away and leave you in peace then, Doctor,' she said. When she shut the door, the din from the post office receded. The glass kitchen door was also shut, but the bulk of Mrs Camerson passed occasionally across it, reminding the priest of a great whale he had once seen circling in the tank at the London Zoo.

'Sit down, Father, sit down.' Magnus pulled out two chairs and sat down to pour the drinks. 'This is not the Ritz but it will have to do. Sometimes when I am drunk enough, I look up from the deal table where I'm sitting and I see those potted palms and ferns against the glass, as stiff as old ladies in mourning. What a place,' he sighed, still referring to the Ritz, 'a tomb for kings.' He wore a collarless shirt with a stud in the top of it, over which the stubble and loose flesh of his chin dropped in folds. 'Health to your parish,' he said, raising his glass.

'Thank you,' the priest said smiling. 'I'll drink to your health too and a long life.'

'I don't want a long life — to tell you the truth it's gone on too long already.'

'So little to live for, have you?'

'So little . . . But we aren't here to discuss my troubles. This is a celebration, you see — two great minds in a little place. Mind you, I'm certain to start complaining some time soon. The pleasure of the lonely is to store up their grievances against the day when

132

they find a really good listener. Now you look like a really good listener.'

Father James started to laugh. The unaccustomed drink had released his tension. Magnus was like a child. 'I am a good listener,' he said, 'otherwise I shouldn't have become a priest.'

'Now,' Magnus suddenly leaned forward so that his nose was almost pressed against the priest's face, 'I am going to ask you an impudent question that I'm certain no one in this village has had the nerve to ask you. Why should a beautiful young fellow like yourself become a priest?'

Father James flushed and folded his hands tightly in his lap. 'But the two things are not connected,' he said quickly. 'They have nothing to do with each other. You might just as well ask an ugly man why he is married.'

'I see.' Magnus was silent for a minute. He turned his glass cautiously around by the stem, between his forefinger and thumb. He looked so much like a ragged bird, perched warily on a fence, which has stolen a crumb and is waiting to see what will happen to it, that the priest began to laugh again. Magnus seemed relieved. 'I'm sorry,' he said. 'I've grown so used to living alone, or at any rate among people who tolerate me, that sometimes I say things I've no business to.'

'I don't mind. The priesthood has an odd effect on people, even the mildest people. I find that they try to shock me. If I'm asked to a dinner party, quite often there will be one or two women there wearing low cut dresses or very short skirts. And then amongst the men, there will be some who swear a bit more than usual or who suddenly attack me on a moral issue they haven't cared about for years. It seems we make people feel guilty,' he said with a sudden beautiful smile, 'even for no reason.'

Magnus pursed his lips. 'That's very true,' he said gloomily, 'very true. I've often noticed it.' Suddenly his face brightened.

'But I will tell you a story now,' he said to the priest, 'in which the opposite occurs. Sometimes you will find a clergyman who takes a real delight in shocking the layman. I used to be a Catholic myself at one time and I had a great-uncle who was a priest.' Father James had now drunk over half a glass of neat whisky, he had a light head and was feeling a little dizzy. The doctor's features were no longer distinct. It seemed as if he were looking at him from the corner of one eye. ' . . . This great-uncle,' Magnus was saying, 'was a Benedictine monk in Dublin — over ninety he was then and with every tooth in his head. Now he was guaranteed, while sitting drinking tea in the monastery parlour with old spinsters, to start telling them of his craving for drink. It was true about this craving, and he couldn't sit down for any length of time without returning to the topic. He would say 'Tea is grand, Miss Flaherty — have another ginger biscuit — but usually about this time of day I am opening my second bottle of claret.' It's a fact, too, that he had at least two crates of good claret under the bed in his cell. Because of his great age, he was allowed as much wine as his relations would send him.

'Anyway the duller,' Magnus said slipping some more whisky into his empty glass, 'the duller the company happened to be, the more terrible his urge to irritate them. When I was a boy of about sixteen I went to visit him once in the monastery, about the usual time for tea. There were three old maiden sisters who subscribed to the church funds there too, and for some reason I now forget, a Protestant pastor, all at the same function. Anyhow my great-uncle behaved all right and for some time, eating up the sandwiches like a lamb and scarcely opening his mouth. He looked old and dim. The three spinsters were delighted, for generally he made them nervous and they were out that day to impress the pastor with this venerable member of the Catholic Church. I was sitting there, meek and bored, my hair was slicked down with brilliantine and I had on my best wool suit. 'It's time I was going,' said the great-uncle in the middle of a cucumber sandwich.' Father James had already started to laugh. 'No, wait,' Magnus said, suggesting a hiccup, 'he stood up, dusting his habit and turned to the pastor with the nicest smile: 'Did you hear this one, Reverend', he said, 'about the Bar Mitzvah? There was a vicar, a rabbi and a Catholic priest . . . ' Now wait,' Magnus said, scratching his head. 'The thing is, I've forgotten the exact story now. But at any rate, no one could stop him and he went right on until he had finished the story, and by the door he thought of another one and told them that too — all in a dead flat voice. And the protestant pastor spilled some hot tea in his lap and the spinsters began to rattle and sway like trees in a gale.' Magnus became more and more Irish as the story went on, and the priest laughed so hard that he banged his elbows on the table in front of him and spilled some of his drink.

At half past twelve Jeanie knocked on the door and came in. 'Excuse me, Doctor, will you be wanting your dinner here?'

'Dinner?' said Magnus. 'Ah' he squinted sideways at the whisky bottle which was now empty. He was still able to calculate that he had drunk three quarters of it himself. Jeanie smiled at the priest. 'Miss Morag will be waiting on you, Father, at the rectory.'

'Jeanie,' Magnus said, 'I shall have whatever your mother is cooking there for your lunch, if you'll be so kind. It will take me just two minutes to drive Father James up to the rectory. We don't want to annoy Morag, do we?'

For some reason, he put his teeth in to drive. It took him some time turning the car in the village street and then he drove at great speed up the road to the rectory, grazing the back bumper against the bridge on his way. Father James held the back door shut with a string over his shoulder.

'This car is ten years old,' Magnus said. 'I can't afford a new one. In general I tie that string to the knob of the windscreen wiper when there is no one in the front seat beside me.' He changed into low gear on the slope of the hill and the car rocked on its axles. 'You must come and see me whenever you like. Don't bother to ring. After ten o'clock at night I'm usually there.'

'I should love to,' said the priest. He realized that he was slightly drunk. A single terrible thought had struck him which brought him close to tears. It was literally months since he had laughed so much. 'I should love to,' he said again. 'I get very lonely here.'

'So you must,' Magnus agreed. They had arrived at the rectory by then but neither of them made a move to get out of the car. 'So you must. I get lonely too, but then, even loneliness wears a bit softer. It doesn't nag any more — you know what I mean.' The priest nodded. 'And isn't that the terrible Morag peering at us through the window? My God, she looks as though she hadn't seen the daylight for twenty years.' Father James began to giggle. He let go the string of the back car door and struggled to get out. 'If I were you,' said Magnus, leaning towards him over the seat, 'I should make out you were as drunk as a barn door. Lurch in there and give her a good fright, why don't you?'

The priest laughed until he had hiccups and could scarcely catch his breath, while Magnus reversed into the garden wall and drove off down the hill in the wrong gear.

Morag turned away from the dining room window where she had been standing for the last half hour. She crossed herself. When she thought of the Devil, she thought of Magnus Laver.

11

For several days Father James avoided the doctor. Magnus had the same effect on him as alcohol: there was a sweet warmth about him, and a peculiar sense of danger. In exactly the same way as strong drink alters the outward eye, confusing and even doubling its vision, so Magnus worked on the inner, setting up a false set of standards and half-truths. Yet the priest in his loneliness felt a longing for the doctor's company and after a while he gave in to it. He set off up the road one night about ten o'clock. It was five miles from Kintillo to Toscaig and he drove slowly and almost reluctantly. The sky was clear after a day of rain. The full moon shone at a slant on the puddles of the road and they were as white and dense as solid ice.

The doctor's cottage looked deserted. No light showed through the windows and the glass shone blind in the moonlight. Father James climbed the steep hill and before knocking on the door he decided to look through a window, hoping to see a sign that Magnus was still about.

There, less than three feet from his own

face through the glass sat Magnus Laver, staring out at him without a flicker of recognition. Nothing in his face moved and his skin was dead white in the light of the moon. Father James started backwards and stumbled against a bucket in the doorway. Angrily he straightened the bucket, and rubbed his shin where he had grazed it on the rim. As he opened the door Magnus started to laugh. 'Did you think I was mummified with drink, Father?'

'You startled me,' the priest said sharply. 'What on earth are you doing sitting here in the dark?'

Magnus rubbed his hands across his eyes and yawned. 'No, the truth of the matter is I nearly got it.'

'Got what?' The priest was feeling about in the mess that littered the tables and chair for some kind of light, a lamp or even a candle. He was sorry by now that he had come. Magnus was still staring out of the window and seemed only half removed from his trance.

'Isn't it always the same?' he said peacefully. 'Just as you are reaching out and the thing is coming at you full face and clear, in this God-forsaken place, where a mouse moving is a big event, someone always has to walk in on you.'

Father James had found a candle and some matches. He lit the candle and set it down in a saucer and then he looked at Magnus. 'And I bet you haven't eaten anything all day,' he said. 'Are you trying to starve yourself to death?' Magnus annoyed him so much at that moment that he searched around for something more insulting to say. 'Look at all those bottles.' He made a sweep with his arm and knocked it against the sharp corner of the paraffin stove. 'At least, if I were you . . . '

Magnus interrupted him. 'How rude of me, Father,' he said, 'I haven't offered you a drink.'

Father James had made a resolution already, not to touch any alcohol that night with Magnus. He had intended to sit there for an hour or so, talking, and then drive home; but he was so irritated by then and the cold was so intense that he took the drink that Magnus held out to him and swallowed three mouthfuls neat.

After he had tipped a whole glass of whisky down his own throat and lit up a cheap cigar, Magnus pulled himself slowly from his chair, and between them they lit the fire, which threw up a choking cloud of smoke, and drew the curtains shut. By the soft light of three candles and the deeper light of the fire, the sharp angles and the squalor of the room dissolved and the setting seemed right as it would nowhere else, for the doctor's strange and lengthy monologues. 'Ah that's good,' he said settling back in his chair. 'My God I don't miss electric light and if it wasn't for the draughts in this place I should call it perfect.'

The priest agreed. He was already ashamed of his previous bad temper and at the same time he was reluctant to destroy the sudden atmosphere of intimacy by apologizing for it. 'When I came in,' he said, 'you were saying something — I've forgotten exactly what it was — you said something about finding it — finding what?'

'Ah,' said Magnus. He shifted slightly in his chair. For an instant he looked coy and this expression on his dissipated face startled the priest. 'Well, I'll try to explain it to you,' he said. 'People ask me periodically why I drink so much. I give each of them a different answer — to keep warm, to keep alive, to die quicker, what have you. The same people who ask this kind of personal question seem satisfied with the same banal answers, you see . . . '

Father James nodded and sipped a little more of his drink. The doctor's voice, the gradual warmth of the peat fire and the pale waxy light of the candles had the same soothing quality in each of them.

'Well now, there are better reasons than that for drinking. I might have used drugs instead, if I could have afforded them.' Magnus leaned forward in his chair. 'But it comes to the same: I need a stimulant these days to get at what I'm after and of course it takes more all the time. I'll try to explain it to you. Do you ever have the peculiar sensation, Father, that you have hold of something, not an idea, but a very perfect dream, a kind of visible ecstasy, and that you just have a hold of it by the corner and say you try to examine it or to keep it there even for a few minutes, that you can't because it won't take the strain; it fades completely and there is nothing left of it but a sense of terrible loss . . . '

Again the priest nodded. He was thinking, 'This is all nonsense, of course.' But at the same time he was mesmerized by the doctor's eyes and voice.

'Well,' Magnus went on, 'if I could only produce this strange kind of rapture when I wanted it and stay with it sometimes for a while as I used to do. For instance, when I was young — still a child — when sometimes I was so unhappy there was nothing and nobody to do anything about it, this unhappiness was often accompanied by a certain picture in my mind, so vivid that I was often able to weep for half an hour as a result of it. And yet it was a meaningless little scene in no way connected with me, of a man in a raincoat walking away down a dark road at night, with his hands in his pockets, hunched up against the rain. This beating rain fell through the lamp-lit circles in the road and overhead the weak light lit up the leaves of interminable plane trees. The stranger was walking away down the road so slowly that he never seemed to move . . . '

Into this, with Magnus half whispering, half sunk already into a coma, and the priest leant forward in his chair staring at him, into this mist of Magnus Laver's great confusion, there came a sudden knocking on the door. The noise was so totally unexpected that the two men sat staring at each other until the knocking began again. The priest sighed and put down his empty glass. Magnus went slowly to the door and opened it. 'Oh it's you is it?' he said. 'If it was anybody else I should have left them out in the cold. Come in, then.' Even before he heard her voice the priest realized that it was Meriel Finlay.

She came quickly into the room, pulling off her headscarf and brushing her hair back from her face. She apologised to Magnus for disturbing him and at the same time she smiled at him gaily. And she was so busy with all of this that she failed to notice the priest until she had sat down.

Magnus hung up her coat on a peg by the door. He turned to offer Meriel a drink and stopped there with his mouth half open. The priest and Meriel Finlay were staring at each other in such a way that, he, Magnus, was now alone in the room. Two things happened at once to him, an intolerable pain attacked him somewhere in the region of his heart, forcing him to sit down quickly in a chair; and at the same moment he thought quite clearly, 'The two of them are lovers. They have been lovers for some considerable time.' Furthermore, he could see the whole evening was planned. Neither of them had come to see him at all. 'Of course,' he said suddenly loudly, 'you both know each other already.'

Meriel turned in her chair. She put her hand quickly over her mouth as though she were covering a smile or even a desire to laugh. Behind her the priest stood up and walked towards the fire, spreading out his hands to the flames, although the room was now so warm that Magnus felt stifled. 'I'm hungry,' he complained. 'I think I need something to eat. In fact I haven't eaten all day.'

'I'll help you,' Meriel said. 'What shall I cook you?'

'Don't trouble yourself on my account. I should hope that I can open a tin without someone rushing to help me. I am definitely not so drunk, am I, that I can't open a tin by myself?'

Meriel shrugged. 'How queer you are tonight,' she said. 'Have I done something wrong? I can't think . . . Perhaps I shouldn't have come. I walked five miles up the road to see you — I thought you would be pleased.'

Magnus ignored her. He went to a cupboard by the sink where he kept cardboard boxes full of whisky. He drew the cork out of one with a sharp twist and drank straight from the bottle. 'Christ,' he said, 'now I needed that.'

But again neither Meriel nor the priest was paying attention to him. Without even looking at each other they were surrounded by the same physical confusion from which he was totally excluded. He watched them for a minute with his eyes narrowed and the whisky bottle still in one slack hand and then he turned back towards the sink where he was standing, picked up a box of matches, opened it and deliberately scattered the contents on the floor. 'Now look what's happened,' he said plaintively. The two of them came across the room to pick the matches up. They knelt down and gathered them together in silence. Meriel was on one knee sweeping the matches into piles, and whenever she stretched forward her hair brushed against the priest's face. And Father James when she touched him, shut his eyes and turned his face slightly towards her. When he straightened up he took Meriel by the arm and helped her to her feet, and Magnus saw too that she stumbled against him, pressing the side of her breast against his hand.

When all the matches were back upon a table in their box, Magnus sat down again and crossed one leg over the other. 'I am going to write this book,' he said at random. 'Have I told you about it, Father?' The priest was staring at the contents of his glass, swilling them around in one hand and when he looked up it was neither directly at the doctor's face nor at Meriel Finlay but somewhere among the shadows of the two of them. Magnus wondered how long it would be his pleasure to bore his two guests. He watched them shrewdly in the same way that a teacher might watch his class towards the end of the lesson, noting whose eyes had strayed towards the classroom clock and who was paying attention. 'I've decided to call this book *The Mindwatcher*,' he went on. 'It will be the study of an alcoholic examining his own brain, you see, watching its gradual dissolution step by step now, from the time that the disease first takes a hold of him, beginning with those great bursts of sunlight that are so beguiling at first, and those dreams which are so rich and bright that you can practically reach out and touch them. And then describing after a time the slow festering of these same dreams, the slow dissolving into nightmares . . . '

The worst of this monologue, the doctor now realized, was that it produced no effect on his listeners at all, not even the desire to yawn. ' . . . Such nightmares,' he went on, raising his voice, ' . . . that presently descend from the head, you see, into the pit of the stomach where they crawl about like worms. Sometimes I have woken up, clutching my stomach, certain that there was a hole there from which these worms were oozing and wriggling out . . . Doesn't this revolt you?' he said suddenly leaning towards Meriel.

'Who me?' she said looking up. She had been picking at the loose varnish on the wooden arm of her chair. With an effort she roused herself and smiled at him. 'I forgot,' she said, 'you haven't eaten yet. Shall I cook you something?'

'She is radiant,' he thought, 'I have never

seen her look so beautiful.'

'Shall I make you an omelette? It won't take me a minute.' Magnus took some more whisky and while he was doing this he stared at her over the upraised bottle. ' . . . or a bacon sandwich — something you really like?'

'No,' he said abruptly, 'no thank you — I'm not hungry any more. I think I'll go to bed now, if you don't object.'

No one made a move to stop him. The other two people in the room were in that strange state which prevented them from understanding anything the doctor said unless he spoke loudly or repeated himself. 'I think I'll go to bed,' he said again.

Father James stirred in his chair. 'Yes,' he said, 'why don't you? I was going to take Meriel home anyway. It's getting late.' He leant forward to blow out a candle, which was guttering in its saucer. It was only the second time he had spoken since Meriel had walked through the door.

Magnus had no intention of going to bed. As far as he was concerned, most of the night was still ahead of him. It was certain now to be a long dull night — and lonely too, intolerably lonely. He felt the same pain as before. It was settling now in the pit of his stomach, merely waiting until the door shut, and in the silence afterwards it would stir up a storm inside him. 'Must you go?' he said suddenly.

His voice was so feeble that Meriel looked at him anxiously. 'Don't you want us to?'

In spite of the way she spoke, Magnus realized that there was no way to delay her. She had made up her mind to leave with the priest. He shrugged. 'Well if you're going to leave,' he said, 'why don't you leave? The fire is going out. The room's getting cold. I shall have to warm it up again when you've gone.'

The priest had already put on his coat and was helping Meriel into hers. In a sense they had already left. He closed his eyes for a second, refusing to think what they might do together once they had shut his door.

'Good night, Magnus.' Meriel crossed the room and kissed him lightly on the cheek. 'I'll come again soon. Look after yourself.' Magnus said nothing. He was watching the priest by the doorway. Even in the warm light Father James looked pale and half asleep.

When they had gone, Magnus stayed where he was for a while leaning against the stove. Suddenly, as though they mattered now, he remembered two things. In one hand, already stiff, he was still holding the whisky bottle. The second was more disgraceful: in the ten years since he had known Meriel Finlay she had never seen him, until that night, without his teeth.

★ ★ ★

Father James drove for a mile or so in silence. It was starting to rain again. Thick clouds flew across the moon, pushed by a violent wind which shook the car and scattered the rain against the windows. Meriel sat beside the priest watching the trees and solitary houses slip past along the road. Each of those that stood out against the night, was a landmark she knew well, and by each she worked out how little time she had left. There was so great a step between her desire and its fulfilment that Meriel sat dumbly in her seat and wondered how it could ever be accomplished. By a flat stretch of empty land between Toscaig and Kintillo, where the steep flank of the hills fell away on one side into a landlocked pool and where the beach came up on the other side to a smooth green lip of grass, Meriel said suddenly, 'Won't you stop the car for a minute before I have to go home?'

The priest cleared his throat. 'Now listen to me, Meriel.'

'I'm listening . . . '

He sighed. He stopped the car by the side

of the road and when he turned towards her Meriel was looking at him, sitting quite still with her hands in her lap. Her scarf was tied too tightly round her head and the priest leaned forward to loosen it. He ran one hand lightly through her hair and around the nape of her neck beneath it. She leaned against him so that he might kiss her, but the priest brushed her skin with his lips — her eyelids, the hollows of her temples and neck, the small round flesh of her earlobe — and this so lightly that Meriel put her arms around his neck and kissed him on the mouth. In that darkness where the blood is pumped faster out of the heart, beneath the skin which inch by inch wakes up, the body burns for use and the brain alone seems to sleep. Meriel heard one meaningless sound in the darkness — the clicking of the wind-screen wipers which the priest had forgotten to switch off.

She unbuttoned her coat so that he might touch her breasts. And she tormented him by leaning her head far back against the seat so that he had another six inches of her flesh to kiss, down into the collar of her dress. While he was kissing her, she took his head in her hands and ran her fingers through his hair. And later she allowed him to undo her dress, which was fastened down the front by an ornamental zip. But the zip caught before it

152

was half way down and here unaccountably Father James turned away from her. He straightened up in the seat and presently he leant forward and rested his head against the steering wheel. In the dim white reflection of the headlights on the road Meriel watched him. She looked at his hair which was ruffled and she listened to the sound of his rapid breathing because these were the extensions of her own desire.

After a few minutes he said, 'Please do your dress up again. I can't look at you.'

For the first time Meriel noticed the cold. The neck of her dress was wide open and the cleft between her breasts was visible above the broken zip. She buttoned up her coat and sighed. 'I wish . . . ' she began.

Father James refused to look at her, even with her coat buttoned up to the chin. He gazed at the road ahead as though the answer to something lay there beyond the beam of the headlights in the darkness. 'I wish it too,' he said. 'I wish we had never met.' They were speaking however of different things. 'I'll take you home now . . . and afterwards you must try not to think of me nor to see me again before you go home. You must forget about me altogether. You must do this for yourself and also for me.'

12

Meriel spent most of her time alone, sometimes walking in the bare hills around the Kintillo valley, taking the long straight paths through the forestry plantations where the larch needles had begun to fall in a steady rain about her feet. Throughout these long walks, she noticed nothing around her. She was totally absorbed by herself and by the priest. She reminded herself continually that from one year's end to the next she would not see him, but her misery at these times would bewilder her because, in spite of everything, it reminded her of an overwhelming happiness.

At least once a day she went down to the post office, and she would settle herself on a corner of the counter between the sweet display and the till. From this position she could see the priest either coming down the rectory hill or walking in the village street. It was remarkable, however, that considering the time she spent there he did not once appear.

Occasionally she would fix the postmistress with a careful look and she would begin to talk in such a way as to draw the conversation gradually round towards Father James. 'I wonder', she would say, 'how any one can stand to be a priest? It must be so intolerably lonely.'

'I don't know altogether,' Jeanie would answer. 'Certain though, it must be lonely,' and she would leave it at that.

On another occasion Meriel said, 'And why should any man give up the chance to have a wife and children? And to lead a normal life?'

The postmistress had never considered such questions as these. 'Surely I nivver thought of it,' she said in a puzzled voice. 'Maybe there are those who don't need such things though, for we're none of us made the same.' Presently she went on with her work.

One morning while Meriel was there, certain to miss Father James again because his car was no longer by the rectory door nor parked in the village street, Magnus Laver came in to the shop. He managed to ignore Meriel although he walked within inches of her to get to the middle of the counter. 'Jeanie,' he said, leaning forward with two rows of his teeth put in for the occasion, 'good morning.'

'Good morning, Doctor,' said Jeanie smiling. She was cleaning the counter with a damp cloth. 'What can I do for you?'

'Since the pub is not yet open, may I

155

trouble you for a quart bottle of pale ale?'

'You'll be wanting to sit next door then. I'll away in there and see if the stove is lit.'

'Don't trouble yourself,' Magnus said gently. 'I'm quite warm enough thank you. Meriel,' he said, turning so sharply that his elbow caught her on the knee, 'will you do me the honour of sitting for a while next door with me? It's a lonely thing for a man to be drinking entirely by himself.'

The shame of her last meeting with Magnus, rose up and practically choked her where she was sitting. She nodded without a word and slid down off the counter top.

'Good then,' the doctor said, rubbing his hands. 'Good, good.' Without seeming to do so, he was watching the beer froth up towards the rim of the mug and feeling in his hip pocket for the flask of whisky which he would later add to spice it up a little.

He held the door open for Meriel behind the counter and followed her into the room, taking care to keep the brimming beer mug steady in his one free hand. Meriel sat down on the window seat with her back to the light and Magnus sat down a little way to the side of her where he could look into her face. He set down the bottle and the mug of beer gently on the table and sighed. That morning Meriel sensed a meanness in him. He had

156

changed in the summer since she came home, there was sharpness, a certain malice in the doctor now which had never been there before. She sat silently with her hands in her lap.

'Well,' Magnus said, after he had taken a good quarter of a pint, 'how long is it now until you leave? A week? Ten days?'

Meriel cleared her throat. 'No,' she said, 'tomorrow.'

Magnus clicked his teeth together and sighed again. 'Ah,' he said, 'tomorrow.'

Hearing these words from someone else, though she had been saying the same thing to herself since the early morning, a blind rush of tears filled her eyes and she stared at the floor while these tears brimmed over and hung to her lower lashes.

'Don't cry,' Magnus said briskly. 'What you need, Meriel, is a course of Vitamin B12 injections — for the nerves, you see. Now the food you eat in this place is insipid stuff — overcooked and without an ounce of real content in it. Not that I eat much myself, but then you don't have the benefit of alcohol do you? Which reminds me . . . ' He removed the flask of whisky from his pocket and slipped a little into his beer. 'Here, have some of this,' he said, holding out the flask. 'It will cheer you up.' Meriel shook her head.

They sat for a while without talking. When she could bear this silence no longer, since it was full of implications, and since Magnus seemed happy to sit there and enjoy her discomfort, Meriel began to talk at random. 'Anyway,' she said, 'Anne will be glad to leave. She has this boyfriend, a student doctor, back in Edinburgh, who's always writing to her. I shouldn't be surprised if he's the kind of man she married — I mean eventually.'

'Mmmmm,' said Magnus loudly. He pinched an ear lobe between his finger and thumb, pulling the flesh downwards until it was stretched grotesquely out of shape.

'She wants,' Meriel went on, turning slightly away from him, 'a neat terraced house in Edinburgh, with a patio at the back, two children and a three-week holiday abroad every summer.'

'Not, I gather, your Shangri-la,' Magnus said, again loudly as if he were deaf and could no longer hear the sound of his own voice.

'No. No it's not. The trouble is I don't know what I want. But it's not that at any rate. That would be like building your own prison, wouldn't it? Did you ever think, Magnus, how many times in one year you could be locking yourself in and out of the same little house — say four times a day,

three hundred and sixty five days a year
— and even away from it you would still be
taking practically the same tracks every time.
You would wear out hundreds of pairs of
shoes on the same pavements, year after year.'

'Some people must earn their living, they
have no choice,' Magnus said heavily. He was
staring at the fireplace, above which there
hung a little wooden plaque that Meriel had
never noticed before. Into the wood of this
plaque had been burned the words: 'Home,
Sweet Home' in slanting print, and the motto
was surrounded by painted roses and stray
leaves. There was a sickly smell of paraffin in
the room from the unlit stove.

'It's the way you were brought up, Meriel,'
Magnus said after a pause, 'by the puritan
aunt and uncle. The straight and narrow was
never any good for those with hot blood in
their veins. In the end, that kind of life is only
something to kick against, a barrier between
yourself and reality. They never teach you for
instance, that there's such a word as money
— stuff to fling around, when you get the
chance, and enjoy a bit. It's a life of toil
behind the net curtains and the money is
saved against the day of wrath. It's a sin to
spend it and a misdemeanour to smile on
Sunday. And the Good Book is entirely
without humour, isn't it? There's no such

159

word in this vocabulary as joy, or even hilarity or even nonsense. My God,' he said, 'when you have no sense of humour, what a steep hill this life must be, don't you think?'

Meriel smiled. 'They're not really as bad as that,' she said timidly.

'Ah, but what fine upright dutiful people. I remember them coming here once to the village store — the only time, to my knowledge, they've been to Kintillo since your mother died.'

'They brought us back from school one summer on their way to Inverness.'

'Yes, well, your aunt marched into the post office before she would put a foot through the lodge gates. 'Is my brother-in-law at home, Mistress Mackenzie?' she said to Jeanie.' Magnus pronounced the word 'Mistress' with a sharp hissing sound which shifted his false teeth. 'Now Jeanie had just the time to nod when your aunt, with a swish of her foxtail attachments, was out of the door again and ordering the trunks and luggage put down in the village street.

' 'Would you like a cup of tea, Mrs Graham?' Jeanie said from the doorway.

' 'No thank you,' said the aunt, halfway back to the car again. 'We haven't the time to wait, have we Thomas?' throughout all this your uncle had never so much as opened his

160

mouth until he said good-bye to you, and they were gone before I had time to get the whisky glass back to my mouth from the counter.'

Meriel looked at him gravely. She was scarcely listening to him, having been there herself at the time, and having heard the story before when Magnus was both drunk and sober. It seemed as if a sudden block of ice had settled around her heart and now when she spoke she was afraid that her words might sound heavy with self-pity. 'You know, in the whole of my life . . . ' she began in a trembling voice. Magnus said nothing, but he focused on her with an odd air of delicacy. 'In the whole of my life,' she repeated, 'I've never seen a photograph of my mother. I can't imagine her. When I think — when I try to see her in my mind, there is just this blank where her face should be, and then, though her hair is short, her body is thin and bony like mine, I've no idea what she was really like.'

'Well,' Magnus said sighing, 'I'm afraid I don't know either. She died before I came here — a good few years before — but I think she did look like you — smaller perhaps, more languorous and plump.' He spread out his hands on the table with the palms downwards, and gazed at them intently, lifting each finger separately an inch or so from the surface. He was passing the time until he could deviate from the subject. 'What I never understood about your family,' he said finally, 'is the rift between them after your mother's death. It's quite beyond me how people can be so foolish. I've never understood whether it was caused by your father or whether it was the aunt' — Magnus spoke of this aunt with bitterness as though she had done him a personal wrong — 'who refused to speak to your father, on account of what,' he added briskly, 'I neither know nor care.'

'Well,' said Meriel. She was moving an ashtray around with the tip of her finger, there being nothing else on the table to fiddle with. 'I think she always held it against him — the way that my mother died.'

'What!' Magnus shouted. He slammed his hand down so hard on the table that the beer bottle jumped and Meriel put out a hand to save it. 'I've never heard so much rubbish in my life — would you credit it? Your poor mother died of a massive haemorrhage after childbirth. Do you mean to tell me that the aunt has arranged the thing in her head in such a way that your father is to blame for it? My God what a wicked, senseless woman.'

'It wasn't quite that,' Meriel said even more

timidly. 'I think she blamed my father for not getting hold of the doctor sooner.'

'So what is she?' cried Magnus, getting more and more incensed, 'a self-elected gynaecologist? What did she know about childbirth, being as I remember totally infertile herself? Huh!' He shook the remaining drops from the quart bottle into his mug with impatience. Meriel regretted having spoken at all. It was typical of the doctor that no sooner had he heard something of this sort, and no sooner had he taken enough alcohol, he became more outraged and more involved in it than the person affected, not only removing from them some of their own just grievances but even putting them into the position of defending the very thing which had made them angry.

'Now look, Magnus,' Meriel said firmly, 'she has never once mentioned the subject. I don't even know if . . . '

'My God, I should hope not,' cried Magnus, again slamming the table. 'Of all the narrow-minded misinformed merciless bitches I have ever in my long life heard mentioned . . . Be so good, my child,' he said suddenly, 'as to fetch me another quart bottle of pale ale from next door — the Whitbread, please. When I hear of such bigotry and

163

meanness it has a terrible effect on my thirst.'

When Meriel came back with the bottle already opened and the froth running down over her fingers, Magnus looked up at her as though she had just come into the room for the first time. When she put the bottle down on the table, he thanked her gravely and swallowed a whole mugful without pausing for breath.

'So,' he said finally, squaring his shoulders and planting his hands firmly on either side of the beer mug, 'it's about time you acquired a taste for a bit of living. You owe it to yourself really.'

'A bit of living?' Meriel repeated. She shifted on the window seat slightly further away from Magnus. 'A bit of living? What do you mean?'

'What should I mean?' said the doctor vaguely. 'Really nothing.' He turned sideways to gaze out of the window and Meriel noticed that he hadn't shaved for at least two days. 'Ah,' he said, 'I see your sister Anne coming up the village street. 'Sister Anne, sister Anne,' he sang suddenly in a strange falsetto voice, 'who do you see there coming down the road in the dust? . . . '

The two of them sat in silence like conspirators savouring the last minutes of a certain freedom. Magnus began to pick his nose, furtively and at the same time stubbornly. Anne Finlay came through the sitting-room door with a firm step. Her eyebrows were raised and her eyes accusing. 'Magnus,' she said briskly, 'I'm sorry for interrupting you. I'm to bring you home to finish packing,' she said to Meriel.

A great draught of fresh air came in through the door behind her and Magnus began to grumble, pulling his coat collar up round his ears. 'The very same as her aunt,' he muttered.

Anne had a hand on her hip and was looking at Meriel in such a way as to say, 'Another minute in this beer-ridden atmosphere will be too much for me.'

'I'm coming,' Meriel said absent-mindedly. She had been struck just then by an idea so simple and at the same time so brilliant that she almost choked with laughter. She gave the doctor a radiant smile and kissed him on the cheek. 'I must go,' she said. Magnus had a hold of her by one arm and refused to let go.

'I was telling your sister,' he said to Anne, 'I was telling her to live it up a bit in the black sour streets of Edinburgh. Get dancing with the students in the bars, why don't you? My God, at your age I was maddened by sex,' he hiccupped. 'Excuse me. And bearing in mind the dull clothes they wore in those days I couldn't look at a pair of pretty ankles without the blood rushing to my head. Are you going then?'

'Good-bye Magnus. I'll try to come and see you before I go.' Meriel was impatient to leave. She longed to be alone now and to study this new idea which had come to her with such suddenness that she felt almost giddy. 'Let's go,' she said to Anne. 'Come on, let's go.'

Magnus looked up at her suspiciously as she left the room, but the sustained effort of staring at Meriel, with both eyes at once, distressed him. As they shut the door, the doctor had begun to sing again in the same weary falsetto as he had used a few minutes before, pulling the empty beer mug round and round by the handle.

13

Every evening Charles Finlay went to bed at ten o'clock, first having bolted the front door and checked the shutters of every ground-floor room. Since it was built in 1720 the house had never once been burgled, but he did these things out of habit. It was part of his army training that he liked every lock and bolt in working order, well oiled and sliding easily into place. It had never once occurred to him that everything he was doing, he had done a hundred thousand times before and always in the same order throughout the long monotonous years.

When the last light on the ground floor had been switched off, he went upstairs to his room, and here half way up the stairs, he stopped and an expression of fear passed over his face. There was a light beneath his bedroom door and this light shone out boldly in the semi-darkness.

In the twenty years since his wife's death, no one other than the housemaids had crossed the threshold of his room. Throughout those twenty years Charles Finlay had built around himself a tight and fussy routine so that one single breach in it caused him the same terror as a normal man would feel when the foundations of his house began to shift beneath his feet.

He walked up the last few steps softly and with one hand in his pocket. He had some wild notion of bringing out his stiletto knife and brandishing this in the face of the intruder. It did not occur to him that one of his daughers was waiting there in the room for him, and when he opened the door and saw Meriel sitting quietly on his bed, he stood rigidly in the doorway and could think of nothing whatsoever to say to her. Meriel also sat without speaking and stared up at him with frightened eyes. 'Papa,' she began.

But the setting was strange to her. Not only the expression in her father's face but the whole atmosphere of the room now terrified her so that the phrases she had been planning throughout the day now stuck in her dry throat. Ever since the morning when she had first conceived her plan, sitting in the store with Magnus, she had put off mentioning it to her father. Each time an opportunity had arisen, she had somehow avoided it. And she had reached, by this indecision, the worst possible moment of all, so that she now sat wretchedly on the bed and stared at him as though she were dumb.

Finlay had meanwhile recovered enough to come into the room and close the door behind him. He took a clean handkerchief from his trouser pocket, blew his nose loudly and rearranged it, without thinking, in the breast pocket of his jacket. He then made an extraordinary remark. 'I hope,' he said repressively, 'that you haven't been meddling with my gun.'

Meriel was astonished. 'Your gun?'

'You must have noticed it,' he went on, 'in the corner over there. It's not loaded but I don't like it tampered with. Besides,' he added, 'fingerprints leave acid marks on the barrels.'

'What do you need a gun for?' she said wonderingly. 'I mean, in here?'

'In the summer the tom-cats come down from the home farm and prowl about the park — you must have noticed them?'

'Noticed them? No, not specially.'

'I find that extraordinary,' Finlay said staring at her, 'considering the noise they make, night after night — and just beneath the windows too when one is trying to get some sleep.'

The conversation now resembled a scene on a darkened stage, in which the dialogue of the principal actors had flown over the heads of the audience and into some dim region of the playwright's fancy.

'I suppose I hear them,' Meriel said after a pause. 'I suppose sometimes I do. But do you kill them?' she asked suddenly.

'Kill them? Certainly I do. Besides the infernal noise they make, they have no business down here in the woods. They disturb the young pheasants.'

'I see.' If she closed her eyes, there was a small vivid picture in her mind: she could see the thin carcass of a cat stretched out in the twilight, pale against the dark grass.

'Why did you want to see me?' Finlay had now sat down on a straight-backed chair by the door and crossed his legs. Meriel began to fidget and she avoided looking at him.

'I don't want to go back to Edinburgh tomorrow,' she said hurriedly. 'I want to stay here, at home . . . '

For the second time that evening Finlay gazed at his daughter as though she were a stranger whose thoughts and actions were quite inexplicable to him. He took so long to reply that Meriel was afraid he had not understood her.

'If I stay here, I could look after you,' she said, 'you and Grandpapa.'

'And do you really want to stay here alone while Anne goes back to Edinburgh?'

'I've spoken to her about it. She doesn't

mind what I do. She's happy to go back. She likes her work, her friends . . . She has a whole life there, while I . . . '

'Well . . . ' Finlay said in a measured way, 'within a week you will be bored.'

'I won't be, I promise you. I shall find plenty to do.' Meriel blushed. For it was here that her thoughts divided into two quite separate streams and they were not even definite enough to be counted as plans. On the one hand, she meant to look after her father, and to keep him company in ways which still remained vague to her, and on the other she wished simply to be near the priest. It was for the second of these two reasons that she now blushed deeply.

Finlay got up and began to walk about the room. Out of his pocket he drew the stiletto knife and drummed this in a military tattoo against the palm of his hand. 'What about your typing course?'

'I've almost finished it — and then . . . well, I could go out tomorrow and get a job as a secretary.'

'I don't think you have the natural efficiency for such a job.' There was no denying it. Meriel said nothing. 'And I suppose you have considered what your aunt will have to say?'

She shrugged. 'I don't think she cares very

much one way or the other.'

Finlay stopped fiddling with the knife and slipped it back into his pocket. 'You would be a fool to imagine it,' he said crisply. 'She has plans for you. I've no doubt she would like to see you with your looks and education, married to a peer of the realm, mmm? Whereas,' he continued, before she could speak, 'here you will have nothing to do and will meet no one.'

'I won't mind.'

'You won't mind?' He seemed incredulous. He stared at her face intently as though he had just then made out certain facts which she was trying to conceal from him. Meriel wanted terribly to cry. The whole conversation from the very beginning, had set off at some crazy slant, and this slant had never been corrected again. It had been foolish of her to imagine her father's delight, or even his interest in her scheme. When she considered it, she had only once in the past summer seen such an expression in his face, and this was when his head keeper, Mackinnon, had trapped and killed in the mouth of the river a great bull seal which was eating the heads off his salmon.

She got up from the bed and straightened up the covers. 'If you don't want me to stay, Papa, I'll go — tomorrow with Anne.' These words, however, sounded clumsy and self-pitying and they seemed also to bring the conversation to a sudden end, so that she was surprised when her father spoke again.

'If,' he said abruptly, 'you would really like to stay, I see no reason why you shouldn't. Some short interval, say, six months or even a year and then we shall see.'

The tears which Meriel had tried so hard to control ran down her face unchecked. And Finlay, at the sight of these tears, immediately withdrew again into his normal state of cold reserve. He managed to push Meriel towards the door, holding her gingerly by one arm, but even this slight contact seemed disagreeable to him. In the open doorway, sensing that she was about to thank him or, even worse, lean forward to kiss him on the cheek, Finlay turned away from her hurriedly and switched on the passage light. 'You had better go now,' he said quickly. 'There's nothing more to be said.'

As soon as he had shut the door and was alone again, he began to walk restlessly up and down the room. At first he was struck merely by the unreality of the situation. He walked up and down the same stretch of floor, bounded at one end by the bed and at the other by the window, and from time to time, he looked up and stared at the familiar

173

objects in the room around him such as the finely carved handles of his chest of drawers, or the frame of a picture which hung above his bed. These things now seemed filled with a fresh significance. The sudden shock had disturbed his sense of balance, sharpening certain faculties and blunting others, so that twice, out of habit, he went to the windows to draw the curtains, and each time he turned away again, forgetting at the last minute why he was there.

While he undressed, he took from his wallet the two photographs he kept of his daughters. Selecting the one of Meriel he stared at it greedily as though he were hoping to find sudden traces of her affection in the blank face which gazed back at him.

And later when he had turned out the light, he lay for some time without closing his eyes. Something strange and almost luxurious disturbed him — a happiness so intense that he treated it warily. This feeling was quite foreign to him. When he thought of it, there was only one occasion in the past few years when he could remember anything like it. And this had been on a morning in late October when there was a heavy frost on the ground. The sun had drawn out the colours of the autumn woods so that every tree and bush seemed to blaze with a cold and brilliant fire. Finlay had taken his gun with him and a new young Labrador, Victory. In the hard-frozen stubble of the open fields, the untrained gun dog had put up a great cock pheasant. Finlay, at a distance of a hundred and fifty yards had raised his gun and shot this splendid bird straight through the chest. And watching his prey fall from the sky in a straight line to the ground, a feeling of pleasure and intense surprise had overcome him. He smiled to himself in the darkness. This was what he now felt, complete surprise — the sense that one had been given a totally unexpected gift. He yawned loudly, turned over in the bed and settled himself to sleep.

14

When Anne had gone, the house settled again into an almost total silence. Outside in the park could be heard the grating cry of the rooks and the changing sound of the sea and the wind, but inside the house seemed empty and almost lifeless. In a number of small ways Meriel missed her sister, and although these ways were negative, for they seldom spoke to each other or did anything together, this loss was unexpected and troublesome.

At first, she had waited for a sense of change to take place in her, for the threads of her three lives, the school, the city and her father's house were drawn together in a single place and now ran on together. But this one life was at times as tedious and undirected as the other three.

After a week of rain, the weather had settled again. The air was unusually sweet and warm, and one morning when Meriel went out, there was a treacherous smell of fresh trodden grass and earth that reminded her of spring. She began to walk, for no reason, towards the home farm. She had noticed that the priest's car was no longer outside the rectory door, and thus the morning, from being lightened by many possibilities, took on a single heavy density so that she was bored already and dispirited.

Some way ahead of her she now noticed a sick sheep lying in the middle of the road. It had been lying there for some time, unable to move and at Meriel's approach, the animal gazed up at her with an expression of suffering that was oddly human. As she stepped around it, she shuddered. It occurred to her that it was about to die and that its great head might suddenly loll forward and brush the side of her legs.

She was twenty yards from the entrance to the home farm and Mrs Mackinnon, the housekeeper, was now coming towards her with a basket on one arm.

'Look at that poor sheep,' Meriel said to her, as she approached, 'someone should put it out of its misery.'

Mrs Mackinnon shook her head. 'It's that softy Morrison,' she said referring to the head shepherd. 'He cannot bear to put a bullet into anything. I have here', she continued tranquilly, 'a nice cake for your father's tea that was freshly baked this morning.' She lifted the lid of a round tin inside her basket and surveyed the brown crust of the cake. 'I always think a fresh cake looks nice. I don't

177

like the cellophane they put on things these days. It gives them the queer unnatural look of the factory.' Meriel agreed. She too looked at the cake which gave off a sharp delicate smell of raisins and warm baking. A question had just then formed in her mind however, and at once it became so urgent that it was out of her mouth before she could stop it.

'Is Father James all right?' she asked. 'I haven't seen him around lately.' Her voice sounded calm enough but she looked now towards the ground and prodded at a pebble with the toe of her shoe.

'Ah now,' said Mrs Mackinnon, 'it's a good thing you mentioned him now, the poor man.' She paused for an instant, as though considering the best way to go on. 'A strange thing happened the other day to Miss Morag,' she began. 'A letter came from Fort William, the first letter she has received, you see, in her life. It was read out to her in the post office. Some cousin was dying there in Fort William — a relation of her mother I think it was, a spinster without a friend, you see, to turn to.' She shifted the shopping bag from one arm to the other. 'Anyway Miss Morag was so pleased with this and never having left Kintillo since the day that she was born, she went straight up the hill to Father James and demanded some money for her fare to Fort William. 'I'm going,' she said. 'The cousin is dying and I'm going. I'll be back when I've nursed her decently into the grave.' And so she went — just like that without fixing on anyone to be looking after him meantime — in her best hat and coat with her clothes wrapped up in a wicker basket and waiting the very next morning for the ferry boat from Kyle.'

Meriel looked at the ground again. She felt both hot and cold. The blood burned in her face and the rest of her body felt numb.

'So I was thinking,' Mrs Mackinnon said placidly, 'myself and Mr Mackinnon, that seeing you haven't fixed yet on a job and besides the grand work you're doing keeping company with your father and the Laird, you could go up there and give a hand to your parish priest from time to time.'

When Meriel looked quickly into her face there was neither irony nor the least suspicion. 'From time to time?' she repeated.

'Myself and Mrs Garvie will take in his washing for the present and look after the church and Mrs Garvie, having less than some of us to do, can spare the time to tidy out his rooms twice a week and take up the provisions. It would be grand for the poor man if'n yourself could cook him a meal or two in the evenings there, when his work is done.'

'Uh huh,' said Meriel.

Sometimes for no more than a second or two, it seems as though the bones of some reality have been quickly and suddenly exposed, although this feeling never lasts and is soon forgotten. It occurred to Meriel while she stood with Mrs Mackinnon in the road that a chain of circumstances had been long ago set up, and nothing at any time had kept her from the priest.

'I'll be going,' said Mrs Mackinnon. She shifted the shopping basket from her left arm back to her right where she always carried it. 'Certain,' she said smiling at Meriel, 'you do lighten the day for your father and for the old man too.'

Meriel flushed and turned away. When she came back from her walk the sheep lay still in the same position in the road. But now its sick eyes were shut and its head was drawn further in upon its neck. When she looked at it more closely she saw that it was dead.

That evening the three of them, Meriel, her father and Sir John sat down to dinner together as usual. There was vegetable soup from a tin, thickened with the same fat beads of barley and onion strips that Mrs Mackinnon threw into every stock she cooked. Sir John spooned it noisily into his mouth, spilling a little of each mouthful down his chin. He gazed directly into the candlelight, sometimes shutting his eyes and leaning towards it as though lifting his face, by an open window, to the heat of the sun.

He had fallen from his bed onto the stone flagged floor the morning that Anne was leaving; and though nothing was broken, the shock had affected his brain, so that patches of his conversation made no sense at all and others were quite displaced in time.

Mrs Mackinnon came in with three lobsters on an oval plate and put them down on the sideboard. 'Fresh, sir, this morning from Danny's boat,' she said as she took away the old man's soup plate.

'Well, last summer,' he said, 'I remember we had two or three of these each and the mayonnaise was fresh then too.'

'That'll be a while ago now,' answered Mrs Mackinnon. She smiled at Meriel as she passed her chair but Meriel, remembering their conversation together in the road, refused to look up for fear of seeing in the housekeeper's eyes a sudden understanding of a different sort between them.

'We used to have proper helpings,' Sir John was saying. 'I remember when we would eat three or four of these lobsters at a time and

181

they were a good size too. I should call these things crayfish,' he said picking one up by the tail and holding it in front of him.

'Is everything satisfactory then?' said Mrs Mackinnon from the doorway. 'You have everything you want?'

Charles Finlay nodded. 'You may go,' he said. 'We'll have our coffee in the study.

'It's always the same,' he complained when the door had shut. 'She overcooks them so that the flesh is invariably tough and tasteless.'

The old man interrupted him. 'Have I told you,' he said to Meriel, 'about the day I swopped a packet of cigarettes for a horse?'

He had told this story many times before; but Meriel now shook her head and asked him to tell her the whole thing again for she had forgotten exactly how it was. Charles Finlay however listened with mounting annoyance as the story lengthened. He couldn't imagine how his daughter managed to look so interested and even now and then to laugh aloud.

Finlay could not abide to hear such anecdotes well told. They reminded him of an incident some twenty years ago which still filled him with shame. As a young subaltern quartered in Stirling Castle he had heard a joke one night in the Mess which amused him enormously. He had taken care to memorize this joke and from time to time he would look out for an opportunity to repeat it. The incident which disgraced him took place in the following manner. One night there had been a large dinner party in the Colonel's house. The food and wines were excellent and all the guests were in high spirits. By the time that the port was handed around one or two of Finlay's brother officers had begun to tell sly army jokes at which Finlay, himself, now flushed with drinking, laughed more uncontrollably than anybody. And then something terrible and unexpected had taken place. Finlay, without realizing any longer what he was doing, had interrupted his commanding officer in the middle of a sentence and began to repeat his joke. And even worse than this he had started with the wrong end of the story first. The point at which he had realized his mistake took on the nightmarish quality of slow motion. The table around him had grown silent. The other guests now avoided looking at him and he could sense among them the same polite hostility that a newcomer would feel on joining a well-organized and close-knit team. And later when looking briefly into the Colonel's face, Finlay had seen a look of total contempt.

In his morbid sensitivity he could still

remember each detail of the evening as though it had just taken place. For this reason he could scarcely wait until the old man was finished and had already interrupted him briskly once or twice to correct certain facts or details in his story.

Meriel, seated between them, was eating the lobster greedily. She took lavish helpings of mayonnaise and scraped the shell with the flat of her fork until it was clean. Whenever it occurred to her, she would lean forward and help her grandfather with his food, extracting fat morsels of flesh from the claws and spooning these into his mouth. Frequently, however, she forgot about him. Her thoughts would turn towards the priest and here her heart began to beat unpleasantly and the distance between them dissolved so that his face was clearer to her than anything in the room around her. At such times she would feel weak and stupid with panic.

'Is it possible,' Finlay said leaning towards her, across his pudding plate, 'just now and then, to have the luxury of a few words from you?'

Meriel flushed and began to fidget with her napkin. He found her silence offensive and seeing for a moment how easily the blood rose to her skin he felt the same quick pleasure that a bully might feel when he had just discovered a certain weakness in his victim. 'Considering', he went on, 'that you have so little to do all day . . . '

'I cleaned out the box-room in the attic,' she answered. 'I found trunks of old clothes there and boxes of rubbish. There were some . . . ' Here she stopped however, for there were silk summer dresses in the attics, cloche hats with fine gauze veils and other paraphernalia that had belonged to her mother. Now thinking of these beautiful clothes, the faint smell of scent that still hung among the folds, and the fine silk that was scarcely worn, she felt a queer sadness in her — a feeling that was sweet and at the same time painful. Throughout the rest of the meal, and later while they drank their coffee together, she talked to her father politely about a number of things which interested neither of them. Besides this conversation there were other thoughts in her mind, entirely unconnected with it and these concerned her mother.

Tucked away among the drawers and cupboards about the house, there were certain objects — notebooks, diaries, gramophone records — which had once belonged to Mary Finlay. No one had thought to throw them away and sometimes Meriel, opening a drawer or a dusty cupboard, and finding them

185

there, would feel a sense of shock as though she had touched for a moment her mother's hand or heard her voice. But these small possessions — the books, the gloves and ornaments — were fragments which merely gave a vague impression of the whole. And it had only occurred to Meriel, while speaking of them, that these boxes of clothes completed an extraordinary and vivid picture of her mother.

★   ★   ★

An hour later, in the dead silence of the darkened house, Meriel crept back down the wide stairs and into the hall. Beneath her father's bedroom door there was still the faint light of a bedside lamp. She passed the next section of the stairs swiftly for this light was something she had not taken into account. Each house in the darkness takes on a new and often frightening character. The ticking in its pipes and the creak of a shifting floorboard, alter at night and become menacing in subtle ways. So Meriel who was only half familiar with these sounds listened fearfully to the soft movement of the wind outside in the creepers, and to the rattle of the landing windows.

In the hall, her slippered feet made a thin

skidding sound on the bare stone and she paused once or twice to look upwards at the point on the landing outside her father's room. It was not yet completely dark. The thickening twilight still filtered through the high windows and centred upon the pale grey square of a mirror by the study door. This was a fine Venetian mirror, weighing half a hundredweight, in which the glass surround was elaborately and beautifully decorated. Meriel was now drawn towards it almost reluctantly as though she were afraid of what she might see there. Among the shadows of the open hall her reflection was indistinct and its details vague and confused. Nevertheless she looked extraordinary. On her head there was a little cloche hat, the veil of which hung down across her face and obscured it so that her body in the dim light seemed practically headless. Below this and around her neck and throat, there were several rows of jet beads that glittered queerly and these fell almost to her waist. She wore a black chiffon dress that was striped with broad bands of silver thread and this too gleamed in an eerie way in the semi-darkness. The dress fell in irregular folds to her knees, and on her feet she wore two grotesque little silver slippers with platform heels. The whole effect was of some mad and loose limbed puppet, prevented only by invisible strings from crumpling in a heap on to the floor.

There was nothing moving about her appearance at all. Neither did it resemble the impression of her mother which she had set out to create. Meriel at once began to giggle and quite extraordinary gaiety now filled her. Still moving cautiously on her platform heels she crossed the hall and went into the study. Here she closed the door gently and switched on the light. In a small cupboard by the fireplace she knew there were kept a number of very old gramophone records. These were all seventy-eights that had at one time been left there by her mother. Meriel switched on the gramophone and knelt down by the cupboard on her heels to examine the records. They were cold to the touch, and unexpectedly heavy. In some places the grooves were worn away and others were badly scratched. And on the labels were a number of orchestras that she had never heard of, and on one particular label was written a strange title: 'The Black Bottom'. Meriel had now reached a certain weakened state in which everything seemed ridiculous to her. The slightest oddity was enough to set her off on a wild fit of giggling. The simple words 'Black Bottom' now struck her as being so amusing that for several seconds she laughed uncontrollably. And again when she slipped the record onto the turntable and listened to the first few bars of the music a fresh outburst of the same wild giggling overcame her. The tune was sweet and catchy however. The saxophone rose up in a great wide beat and below it, like the second thread of an interlinked chain, the piano followed.

Gradually the music completed a certain mood in her that had been missing all the evening. She felt calmer somehow, and her senses had loosened so that its rhythm now started to flow throughout her body. Presently she turned the record over and began to dance languidly to the tune of a slow foxtrot. Her chiffon dress moved in the same gentle rhythm and the jet beads around her neck clicked one row against another in the cleft between her breasts. In the middle of this scene, at the point where the music had reached a certain plaintive crescendo, Charles Finlay walked into the room. Over his pyjamas he wore a strange-looking dressing gown, gaudily patterned in a paisley print, and his feet were clad in Moroccan slippers with long pointed toes. It seemed to Meriel as she stood and stared at him, that she took in these details with a startling clarity.

For several minutes there was a total silence and in the space of this silence Meriel and her father were both suspended. Deep in the sidewoods a night bird called out in its flight through the trees and the sound could be clearly heard inside the room. There were two dull spots of colour on Finlay's cheeks and the rest of his face was pale. His eyes seemed to travel in a straight line from the absurd cloche hat to the silver slippers. Meriel closed her eyes and waited while her father watched her intently from the shadows by the door. In her face he could see the same mute resistance which reminded him of her mother long ago, and this resemblance was so strong that he confused them both for a minute in his mind. 'You are nothing but a slut,' he said distinctly.

Meriel slid down off the arm of the sofa where she had sat down, and smoothed out the creases in the chiffon dress. She walked around her father towards the door, in the same lazy unhurried way that she normally walked. She swayed her hips a little as she passed him, so that the folds of her dress brushed for a second against his legs.

She stopped for a moment in the open doorway and Finlay now felt a sharp rush of cold air from the hall. 'Good night,' she said abruptly. 'When I've changed I'm going out.'

15

She had nothing planned. Her rage had gone now leaving her frightened. There was no time to imagine what she would say to the priest when he opened the door. And with the light behind him, she would lose the expression in his face, and judge nothing by it, whether to go in with him or leave.

She turned to look back down the hill. The cold and the sea-mist were so dense they seemed made of a single solid material which caught in her throat and stifled her. The village lights were out by half past ten and the house was hidden by the side-woods in the valley. Below her the sea crept out so gently down the beach, it might have frozen there in patterns to the sand.

'If there was a single light down there I'd go home,' she thought, 'and if he opened the door before I reached it, I should be caught here half up and down the hill.' The light above the door was out. The house looked deserted and when she touched the bell, the noise seemed to spring alive under her hand and to echo afterwards inside her head. When Father James opened the door she was standing there staring at him, frozen and dumb. He stood in the open doorway and the light behind him fell full on Meriel. He leant against the side of the door with his arms folded across his chest and he stared at her as though he had never seen her before in his life. He was strangely dressed, in jeans and a frayed check shirt. The sleeves of his shirt were rolled up above the elbows, there were fine blond hairs on his forearms and above the open loose opening of his collar.

Meriel pulled the muffler down from her face. 'I came to see if I could help you — with the dishes and things . . . '

The naked light bulb in the hall behind him shone directly in her eyes, and while she looked at it, this light seemed to swell and grow brighter and brighter until he was nothing but a shadow between them. 'If I've come too late, I'll come back some other time . . . '

'No,' he said slowly, 'now you're here you'd better come in out of the cold.'

She followed him into the narrow hall and while she took off her coat and the muffler from around her neck, he gazed at her without any expression in his face. Meriel began to talk hurriedly. 'Is this your kitchen?' she said, pushing open the swing door. 'What a mess. I should have come before. I only

192

heard about Miss Morag this morning . . . '

'Why didn't you go back?' he asked.

She looked up at him quickly. 'Did no one tell you? I decided to stay. I wanted to stay here.'

Father James was hanging her coat up on a peg in the hall. He turned when she spoke to him and looked at her steadily for a minute. In his eyes she imagined a total understanding but almost immediately his face was vacant again, and sleepy as though he were thinking of nothing at all. He looked at her body in the light through the kitchen door. Meriel wore cotton trousers on a cold night and a jersey which was shrunken and matted from over-washing — the sleeves were too short and the front of it dragged against her breasts. The trousers had also shrunk so that the elastic of her knickers showed plainly underneath and the priest considered all this in a slow and unfamiliar way as though they shared a secret together which had just then been formed. The atmosphere in the room reminded Meriel of those nightmares in which her body moved weightlessly, and where each step forward left her motionless and in the same place. She went towards the sink, and Father James leaning against the door watched her while she stacked up the dirty plates and dishes into a bowl. A piece of cold spaghetti slipped from a plate on to the draining board and she picked it up carefully with a fork and scraped it into the dustbin underneath the sink.

'Tell me about nineteen-year-old girls,' he said suddenly from the doorway. 'I don't know many. I wish I had a sister of about your age. I should like to know if many young girls get dressed up in trousers as tight as those and go out at night to look after the village priest.'

Meriel said nothing. She washed each plate very carefully and put it in the rack to dry. She licked the side of her cheek where a tear was sliding down towards her mouth. Father James left the doorway and came over towards the sink. Behind him the swing door creaked shut. 'But I never realized before,' he said in the same gentle voice, 'how unselfish you are. When I think about it you've given up so many things, your friends, your work, even your boyfriends — because I'm certain you do have boyfriends — and you've chosen to stay here in this dead end place. But now you are free, as it turns out,' he added softly, 'to help me here.'

'I stayed here to look after them — my father and grandfather — to keep them company.'

'I see.'

'Besides I hated Edinburgh,' she said in a whisper. The plates were now washed up and she turned to the dishes.

'So you did. I was forgetting that.' He picked up a dishcloth from the side of the sink and one of the plates from the drying rack. 'Would you like me to help you?' he asked. 'It's a good thing you came really. I'm very grateful. Mrs Garvie has had 'flu for the last two days. But I expect you knew that already.'

Meriel shook her head. The tears fell down her face so fast she could no longer see what she was doing and the dishes had begun to swell monstrously in the bowl and to slip about in her hands. She thought that if he would only move — even a foot or two to the side — she would be able to get to the door, but he was standing so close behind her that she could feel the heat of his body through his clothes. While she was thinking this, that she would never speak to him again, nor walk up the road to hear mass in his church, nor eat again at the same table so long as he was dining there, the priest said suddenly in a different tone of voice, 'Are you crying? Don't cry, please don't cry.'

He put his hands on her shoulders and pulled her round in such a way that she fell against his chest. While she cried there for a little, noisily and without control, he stroked her hair and patted her gently on the back. 'Don't cry,' he repeated over and over again, 'don't cry.' The matted wool of her jersey clung to her skin. Suddenly the priest sighed and pushed her away from him. 'Come and sit down,' he said. 'I'll make you a strong cup of coffee — the way Magnus makes it.' He spoke to her now as though she were a child, leading her towards the table and pushing her gently down into a chair. He went to the sink and filled a kettle and while it came to the boil, he watched her intently until her shoulders had stopped shaking and she sat quietly at the table. Then he left her and went to the cupboard under the stairs where the drink was kept and he brought back a bottle of whisky, slipping a little into each mug and setting them down on a corner of the table. Meriel watched him listlessly. Now and then she gave a deep sigh which was all that was left of her storm of crying.

He sat down and pushed a mug towards her. 'Come on, drink it,' he said. 'It will do you good.'

She ignored him. Though it no longer mattered, she was wondering how much of her mascara had washed off around her cheeks and mouth. She made a triangle in the crook of her hand with some crumbs that were on the table.

'Listen to me . . .' he began. She wondered what kind of a fool he must take her for, since there was nothing he could say which would soften her.

'I have to go now,' she said politely.

'Wait till I've said what I have to say and then you can go. I have the only job in the world,' he went on, 'which finishes here tonight if you stay with me — I can't get up tomorrow and go on with it.' His hands were clasped so tightly around his cup that they were red and must have burned from the heat inside it. He was sitting there very quietly as though he had only that moment understood what he was saying and Meriel felt a sudden intense pity for him. This feeling was both violent and fragile and its strength astonished her. She put out a hand and touched him lightly on the arm.

'I wish . . . ' she began. She would have liked to explain it to him — this and other things besides, that now seemed suddenly quite clear to her — but the priest had sprung to his feet and started to walk rapidly up and down the room.

He told Meriel to go home; that he found her beautiful and even desirable and wasn't this enough for her; that if only she would go home she might think of him alone there and miserable without her. He said that it was time he fetched her coat and took her back and yet, on his way to the door, he changed his mind. He turned sharply before he reached it and went on walking up and down the same stretch of floor between the table and the sink.

Meriel watched him placidly, sitting sideways in the chair. She was no longer afraid of him nor of anything they might do together. She heard the tap dripping in the sink and beyond it the sound of a sudden wind that was lifting along the shoulder of the hill and moaning between the window frames. These things appeared to her like the first signs of the storm into which she walked as she went with light steps towards the priest.

This storm seemed to lift them both from separate corners of the room towards each other and at its centre there was a sudden blindness.

★   ★   ★

When he had taken her up the stairs however and had closed the door of his room, the priest turned away from Meriel and would not look at her. Beneath her bare feet she felt the cold of the lino floor. For the rest, she felt nothing beyond the simplest emotions — a

198

strong desire for him and a certain boldness. She began to undress calmly and without hurrying. She pulled the jersey over her head and then the shirt in such a way that her breasts, once freed, lifted in a single pure movement beneath her upraised arms. And afterwards she shook out her hair so that it fell in a mass about her shoulders. All this she did with a certain easy grace of which she was totally aware.

The priest, from his position by the door, now turned and gazed at her naked body. He looked at it in the same grave way that he might have considered a long awaited present, delivered to him and duly unwrapped. He stretched out his hand and stroked the skin of her arms and breasts in a slow deliberate way and then, as though a certain tension was now released in him, he pulled her body towards him and began to make love to her.

There was a certain shape to the time that followed. Just as the last daylight gave way to the cold beams of the rising moon, and in the same slow fashion returned, so the night between Meriel Finlay and the priest passed through three particular stages. For some time they made love and were aware of nothing in the room around them; later they talked for a while; and again, before leaving, they made love.

Violent lovemaking — like the two acts of birth and death — takes place in an almost total darkness, so that afterwards these sensations are inexpressible and there are only certain details which remain. The angle of a hand against the window, the taste of salt on the skin — these details are vivid and confused.

And there is finally the bewildering sense that the body, from a single firm place is pitched into a wide and turbulent darkness. All these images afterwards passed through Meriel's brain like scenes formed quickly on a darkened screen. They were without sequence or even a fixed place in time.

Presently, while they lay quietly together in the bed, she looked around the room. She took in the narrow cupboard, the faint pattern of the shabby curtains and the exact slant of the moonlight across the open floor. It seemed to her that by fixing such simple details in her mind, she would come to terms with her own astonishing happiness. But having said to herself, 'This is how it is: the bed here, the clothes in a heap beside it, the table over there and the bedside lamp,' her sense of unreality remained. The room was cut off from her normal life. She could neither imagine it now in the daylight nor the priest alone there again without her.

He leant on one elbow on the pillow and the bed was so narrow that half of his weight was resting against her. He played with her hair, combing his fingers through it and arranging it in such a way that it spread out like threads of a loosely woven material against the pillow. The moonlight had drained the room of colour. The pillow was a startling white, and her hair laid out across it was black and without inflections.

'I noticed your hair,' he said. 'First your hair, and then your body.' He paused and smiled at her. 'And later your face.'

'In that order?'

'In that order.'

She smiled back at him. 'And do you still?'

'No,' he said simply. 'Now you are all of one piece to me.' He lay down again in the bed and closed his eyes. 'The other night, I sat down to write to you. I was lonely. I started to write you this letter . . . ' Here he stopped. And when she asked him what it was he had written, he told her there was nothing, nothing of any importance and later he had torn up the letter.

She ran one hand across his body. The skin was damp for he had made love to her with a strange intensity and she could feel the speed at which his heart still beat.

'Listen,' she began. She was filled with a sudden tenderness towards him. This tenderness was deep and heavy and though she searched for them, she could find no words to express it. Nor did he listen. He stroked her hair away from her face and lightly kissed her in the hollow of the neck where the skin was warm and the pulse beat strongly beneath. He did not refer again to the past. They made no plans to meet again, and they behaved as though a time beyond the limits of the room did not exist.

In this strange state, almost nothing disturbed them. From time to time they listened to the sound of the wind outside in the night, and through the window they watched the progress of the moon. Meriel looked up at one time, and saw it suspended from the middle of a single pane, so fierce a light that the stars around it were almost invisible. But later when she looked again the moon had gone and the sky was almost light.

★   ★   ★

It was five o'clock in the morning when the priest took Meriel home down the road. Across the sky, driven by a high wind, thin shreds of cloud passed over the moon, and the same wind rattled in the trees and slammed at the rectory gate. The sea came in at a south-west slant across the sound and the full path of the gale struck a corner of the bay as they were coming down the hill. The priest had an arm around Meriel's shoulder. Long strands of her hair worked loose from her head scarf and whipped against her cheek.

'Let's run,' she said. 'Come on, let's run down the rest of the way.' He couldn't hear her for he sheltered her and the warm wind drummed in his ears. When they came to the bridge, he stopped there and pulled her back against the parapet.

'I have to leave you here,' he said. 'Will you be all right?' He unbuttoned her coat and slipped his arms around her waist. He tasted the salt in her skin and in her hair. Below them the river beat against the arches of the bridge and the spray flew across the road. 'I have to go,' he said again.

Meriel stretched up and put her arms around his neck. It was neither the same night she had stood on the rectory doorstep, nor the same place. Between the two occasions she had gone through a great span of time. She asked him no questions. She was concerned with nothing beyond the next few minutes: in the force of such happiness it seemed impossible that she should put one foot in front of another and walk away. But the priest had begun to loosen her arms from around his neck and at the same time to distract her from what he was doing by stroking her face and kissing her. Presently he asked when the next dance took place in the village hall. Meriel did not immediately see the sense of this. She was startled. 'You mean the ceildhe?'[1] she answered. 'There's one on Saturday night. Why? Shall you come?'

He smiled at her. 'Why? Would they have me?'

She shook her head. 'You can meet me afterwards. You can meet me here.'

'No, not here,' he said after a minute. 'Out in the side-woods.'

'By the wooden bridge.'

'Yes — there then. On Saturday night. Now you must go.' She kissed him once on the mouth and released him. He watched her running away towards the wall of the park. She ran with erratic energy like a happy child and her coat flapped loosely behind her in the wind. She waved to him from the top of the wall and then she slipped down on the further side and was out of sight.

When she had gone, Father James did not immediately turn and go back up the hill to the rectory. Some time ago in the course

---

[1] Pronounce ceildhe as caillie.

204

of the night he had reached a decision, and this decision had come to him in an odd manner. It had appeared to him fully formed and with a certain air of menace, as though a third person in the room had spoken the words aloud. And now this feeling of menace was accentuated by the queer half-light of the dawn and by the raging wind. In this unnatural light was the same effect that is found in the last thin rays of sun before the clouds of a coming storm, and the wild movement of the trees was scarcely separated from the darkness of the hills behind.

Father James now turned, and scarcely realizing what he was doing, he walked down towards the beach facing full into the path of the wind. For a few minutes he stood looking out to sea. The tide was coming in and the waves formed a wide straight line like a wall across the mouth of the bay. 'I'm leaving,' he said aloud, and having spoken these words he felt a sudden extraordinary weakness. The beauty of the sea in front of him and the happiness he was giving up were now confused in his mind, so that Meriel Finlay and the country he was leaving became the two parts of a single terrible loss.

When he turned to go back up the hill, the

morning light was already visible above the high ridges of the Torridon hills. Behind him as he walked up the road, the first sounds of the village morning were carried past him on the wind.

16

On a Saturday night, the last week in September, Meriel went to the ceildhe with her father.

When the Laird was young and the village hall was newly built, there had been a ceildhe once a month, and a band to play the reels. And young girls from as far away as Inverness had won prizes there for the sword dance and the eightsome reel.

But that was more than fifty years ago and in the time between, the ceildhes had become smaller, dingier affairs. Now when the beat of the music reached a certain pitch the paper decorations descended on the heads of the dancers and when the liquor ran out, the village people went home instead of staying to sing as they used to until the morning came.

At one time an element had crept into these gatherings that was foreign and destructive. For several summers in a row, a gang of youths had come over the pass from the council houses of Strathcarron. They swaggered on the dance floor in their dirty jeans, ran pocket combs through their hair in front of the local girls and sneered at the boys dressed up in kilts. There was one, Jim Garvie, whose hair was greasier and whose jacket was heavier with studs than all the rest, and he was the leader of this gang. He taught the girls how to jive to the music of the eightsome reel. He snapped his fingers and shook his hips and danced alone in the middle of the floor. One night while there was singing in the hall, Jim Garvie took a young girl out among the dock leaves and the long grass at the back of the hall and made her pregnant. In those days which are now history, he was made to marry the girl by her father and two friends. They took him out again to the same long grass at the back of the hall and they beat him until he was senseless, for the rise and fall of the singing through the open windows covered every cry of protest. Now this gang no longer came in the summer time; the ceildhes were peaceful again, and yet there was a certain small fraction of the village who missed the air of tension that the greasers had taken away with them.

Meriel and her father went on foot to the ceildhe. 'It will reek,' Finlay said, 'of whisky and cheap tobacco in the hall. We shall need all the fresh air we can get on the way home.' They walked down the drive and along the beach road in silence. It had rained all day and a mist rose up knee high from the ground. Several times Meriel, in her galoshes, walked into puddles and the mud spattered up around her legs and the hemline of her dress. 'You should have worn gumboots,' Finlay said.

Once a year he dressed up like a fool in full dress tartan and he went to the ceildhe as his father had done before him, and his grandfather before that. He wore the same lace jabot handed down, and the same velvet jacket with square silver buttons on the front and sleeves.

It was a beautiful night after a hard day's rain. There was a hush in the air on which the music of the ceildhe stretched out faint and thin like a strange lament. Alone, Charles Finlay might have walked on his way, down to the water's edge while the tide was out, across the paths of the river mouth which he knew so well that he could cross the sand on the darkest night without once wetting his feet. A gentle wind came in across the water and he lifted his face towards it as a blind man might turn his eyes towards the heat of the sun. All this time, he was conscious of Meriel walking silently beside him and of his dullness which cut him off from her and made him seem ugly. As they walked up the steps of the village hall, he took one long deep breath of the night air before he followed her through the door.

There was an eightsome reel in progress. The windows of the hall were entirely steamed up and the bare wood boards shook to the pounding of the music. It took some time for the village people to notice that the Laird's son had arrived. In those few minutes, Finlay wore the cold expression of someone who had a disagreeable duty to perform and intended to get through it as quickly as possible.

When the music stopped, however, and the floor began to clear, something humiliating took place which he had neither remembered nor envisaged. Little by little, the talking and the laughter died away. One face after another was turned towards the doorway. Small groups of people close to him, broke up and flattened themselves against the wall. And they were not looking at his pretty daughter, who was only waiting to be noticed and asked to dance. The entire hall focused like some great collective eye upon Finlay himself, and this eye neither approved nor condemned but seemed to isolate them both and pin them back against the wall. The silence lasted for perhaps thirty seconds, but in this time Meriel looked ready to cry and Finlay was conscious of a fine cold sweat on his hands and forehead.

The factor now came forward a little too eagerly and stumbled against a chair leg as he approached. He wore a fixed look of gaiety. This look, put on at the entrance to the hall, was the same that he wore on every similar occasion. Beside him his wife began to speak about several different things at once. While she was shaking hands with him she admired Finlay's lace jabot, the nice playing of the three-piece band and Meriel's pretty dress, in the same rushed sentence.

Meriel, like her father, now wore an expression of proud indifference and when they were taken to their seats against the wall, she settled herself on the edge of the chair and stared mulishly in front of her. The factor Jefferson and his wife sat down beside them.

Jefferson had a certain working relationship with his employer and one on which he prided himself. It was a delicate balance between his superior knowledge and training on the one hand and Finlay's authority on the other. So long as they were both confined by the farm office or within the grounds of the estate this balance was maintained. But directly they met socially, Jefferson gave way to an almost uncontrollable panic. He could think of nothing whatsoever to say. Even worse than this, his wife chattered on in a gushing way that humiliated him. He now sat besides his employer rubbing his hands violently together and he could hardly screw up five decent words into a sentence.

The music started up again. It was a foxtrot which no one had played south of the border in the past ten years. Danny the Lobsterman's two daughters walked out on to the floor and began to dance languorously together, neither one looking the other in the face, nor speaking. Presently a young shepherd selected the fattest girl in the room and danced with her in a curious swooping movement as though he were trying to lift her and carry her bodily across the room. Gradually the floor filled up. But the dancers, in the main, were middle-aged and most of the younger men stood around the bar at one end of the hall. They stood there awkwardly as if their bodies were better suited to the swaying of a boat or their feet to the mud of ploughed fields. The very old men sat silently, smoking and drinking. When they looked at the dance floor at all, they stared with complete indifference at the couples moving round it.

Presently the factor, seeing an opportunity to escape, blew his nose noisily once or twice and stood up to ask Meriel Finlay for a dance. Meriel, who had been staring moodily at the band a moment before, now rose in a swift graceful movement and gave the factor her arm. Finlay, glancing just then in her direction, surprised in her face a look of sudden gaiety as though the atmosphere of the evening had changed from one moment to the next, and from being intolerably dull, was now filled with promise.

Charles Finlay was now alone. The two seats either side of him were empty. He had two alternatives. To remain where he was until Meriel returned or to walk back towards the entrance where a gathering was centred round the bar. The second of these two he did not consider for he was never at ease with his subordinates. He was a man they preferred to visit together in twos or threes. Whilst they were with him they were careful to speak in generalities and he would feel in them a simple animal antagonism which further increased his own reserve. So now he could not go up and drink with his tenants at the bar nor pretend, besides, a camaraderie which he did not feel.

In the course of the evening Finlay danced once with his daughter, a foursome reel, and later a waltz with his housekeeper Mrs Mackinnon. Finlay was a fine dancer and a good-looking man. His back was straight and his footwork both neat and self-assured.

From time to time, as he danced, a brief look of pleasure would cross his face, but this look was gone again almost the instant he sat down.

One thing, however, alleviated the long and tedious evening. Meriel, in the last two hours, had scarcely once sat down to rest. She danced every dance with a different partner and there was an extraordinary radiance in her which her father had never seen before. Gradually Finlay was aware that she was the centre of attention. Whenever she stood up to dance, there was an imperceptible tightening in the atmosphere. The crowd at the bar would shift and regroup in such a way that they could get a better look at the dance floor. And each of her partners in turn seemed to sense a special warmth in her, which they responded to. Now the competition was not fierce. With the exception of Meriel there were scarcely two women in the hall of passable good looks. Nevertheless Charles Finlay felt an intense pride of ownership and of achievement and wherever she was in the room his eyes repeatedly strayed towards her. At such times his whole face would soften and his body would briefly relax.

When Meriel sat down at last beside him, she was flushed from the heat in the room and her arms and shoulders drooped with exhaustion. She turned to smile at him. And this smile indicated that she was exceptionally happy, that she found the whole evening delightful and loved everyone around her. 'Wait,' she said, catching hold of his arm. 'In a minute now Danny will begin to sing.' But when he started to answer, Meriel had already turned away from him and was waving to someone across the hall.

The three musicians were drinking neat whisky and their accordions lay on the ground at their feet. There was a general unrest in the hall and in that sudden quiet after the shouting and stamping of the reels there was nothing whatsoever to do.

There comes a time, at a good ceildhe, when just so much is drunk and out of this a certain mood builds up — a sweet regret for the times which are past and finished with. Then after a while, softly, and almost for himself alone, someone will start to sing. Three people in the villages could sing in such a way that a listener would feel a chill run along the length of his spine and a certain emotion rise up in him that was at once gentle and bitter. One of these singers was Mary Lee Macdonald.

Sometimes the first few notes she sang were hesitant and at other times her voice rose up easily and clearly from the silence. Sometimes she sang alone for as much as half an hour and at other times the lobsterman sang with her and the songs they sang were almost always sad.

They have memories there which go back beyond their lives to a time when the living was easier and the land was rich with cattle and good crops. Mary Lee and the lobsterman would sing of the years before the sheep destroyed the lands. They would sing too some nights of the islands that are out of reach across the waters and of long journeys which ended in loneliness and death.

Mary Lee sang alone that night, the song of the Whirlpool Corrievrechan and the great tide races of Camuslang and the same waters of the Minch in which her husband, a fisherman, had drowned five years before. While she was singing, Charles Finlay felt something rise up in his chest which sickened him. His throat was constricted and at the same time the rest of his body felt weak and fluid. Blindly he turned from the singer's face and fixed his eyes on an empty corner of the room. But presently his mood settled again and he began without thinking to bite his nails.

When Mary Lee stopped singing it was

past midnight and for a while no one spoke. Then gradually the village people began to shift about on the hard-backed chairs and the dreaming slipped out of their faces. They waited for the Laird's son to leave.

17

They had been standing for some time now, Meriel and the priest, among the trees that bordered the river. Leaning against the thick trunk of an oak, their bodies left a single shadow on the ground, that was sometimes detached from the tree and sometimes melted into it. For a long time they scarcely spoke, and the priest, with his eyes closed, stroked Meriel softly and lazily beneath her coat, and with his mouth he explored the skin of her neck and face.

Meriel had this effect on him, directly he had seen her coming towards him, a pale slight figure in the darkness of the woods, he had forgotten entirely the reason for their meeting. And now when he loosened his hold on her and looked down into her face, it was impossible to speak to her of the things which were in his mind.

Father James was a gentle man. He had a fear both of hurting and being hurt. Once as a child he had witnessed a fierce argument between his parents. He had stayed in the room out of a simple terror that their anger, like an undirected wind, would veer suddenly towards him if he moved. The argument had leapt from one subject to another, continually finding fresh aspects on which to feed itself. And finally his mother, with a cry of distress, had run from the room with her hands over her face. It had seemed to him at the time that something senseless and cruel had taken place. He could not forget it.

Meriel's face was now upturned towards his. Even in the half light he could see the happiness in her face. It now seemed brutal to destroy this happiness so soon after meeting her. 'Tell me about the ceildhe,' he said softly.

'The ceildhe,' she answered. 'Well, it was like this . . . ' She too seemed distracted, however, and did not complete the sentence. Her movements were drowsy and slow. With one finger she brushed his eyelids, and then his mouth. 'I danced with the lobsterman,' she said presently, 'the lobsterman Danny . . . I wish you could see him . . . And then later,' she added, as though remembering events which had taken place some years ago, 'later, they began to sing . . . and the singing was really beautiful.'

'Is there only one lobsterman?'

'Only one. It doesn't pay.'

A bright moon was rising over the bay and it lit up the open fields and the fringes of the wood with a strange greenish light. It cast shadows so faint across the valley that they were like patches of darker earth on the pale ground.

Over the priest's shoulder Meriel gazed out across the field. This look at first was wide and vague but suddenly her attention sharpened. Something had moved in the flat cold light of the open valley. 'Look,' she said quickly. 'Someone's there.' The priest straightened up and turned around. 'I thought I saw someone there — by the road,' she repeated.

In the moonlight however, the road was indistinct. He could see nothing beyond a thin black line of trees that ran along the farther wall. He leant back against the tree. This interruption had startled him and brought him to his senses. In a short time he was leaving her. A temporary post in the Salford Diocese had been found for him by his cousin. The place and the date were already fixed and yet he had told her nothing. His heart began to beat at an increased speed. 'Meriel,' he said quickly, 'listen to me.'

Meriel smiled and shook her head. She took his face in her hands and began to kiss him on the mouth with small, rapid kisses. But a moment later, something in his manner, or perhaps in the tone of his voice, disturbed her. Suddenly she cried out, 'Ah don't — don't speak — don't say anything.'

Father James gave in to her without resistance. He pulled her around towards the tree and pressed his body against her. At the thought of leaving her a furious rebellion now overcame him. With increasing passion and confusion, he now spoke to her of many things which he had no right to mention, and he made her certain promises, too, which he would not keep.

⋆ ⋆ ⋆

The two people in the wood were not alone. Below a dry stone wall which separated the wood from the open fields, a figure crouched among the shadows, and silently listened to them. The night was very still. The air seemed liquid under the moon and all the sounds in it were softened. At times the two voices were audible, but at others they sank to a slow murmur. And this murmuring became confused with the steady movement of the river through the trees beyond.

Miss Morag had been crouching for some time against the rough stone wall. Corn stubble pressed sharply through the cloth of her coat and into the flesh of her stockinged legs. Besides this she was cramped from sitting doubled up in the one position and her coat was damp from the raw ground. She scarcely noticed these things, however, for a peculiar exhilaration filled her. Her heart beat so loudly she was frightened of the noise and pressed her arms across her chest to stifle it. For a while she was content to remain with her head below the level of the wall and merely to eavesdrop. For she was also afraid of the moon's strength. It shone directly across the top of the wall and with a queer intensity. Presently the two voices became increasingly hard for her to hear and Miss Morag became restless.

Little by little and with infinite patience, she raised her head above the wall so that her eyes were on a level with the topmost stones. And here, not ten feet away from her, was a sight that made the housekeeper catch her breath. Among the last trees of the wood, and clearly visible against the broad trunk of an oak, the figures of Meriel Finlay and the young priest were deeply embraced. But it was not this which filled her with a sudden and unexpected heat. It was the stance of their two bodies against the tree; for the priest, with his back to her, now moved in a steady and vigorous rhythm against the young girl's body in the same rough manner — she now remembered — as the farm bulls would rut in the open sunlight of the fields.

Her breath came in short gasps and her knees below the level of the wall were shaking. Her eyes became fixed in a dark sweet craving on the priest and when he cried out at last as though in pain his cry seemed to flow out from the depths of her own body. She clung to the top of the wall to prevent herself from falling down beside it, but the violence of her excitement was now too great for her and she sank down again amongst the shadows, shivering and suddenly confused. She lay there, almost supine, until the last bewildering sounds had ceased and the silence of the night had returned. Above her, the moon, scored by the blunt stubble of the corn, continued to shine indifferently on her upturned face.

18

Miss Morag had a memory which was childlike and under-developed. By the following morning she had entirely forgotten her own strange behaviour and thought only of the incident between Meriel and the priest. This scene took place in her mind in black and white and its details had the sharply-focused clarity of a photograph. She now had enough evidence stored up against Father James to have him hounded from Kintillo.

For a long time she had spied on him. At first these activities had given her a new interest in life and for a while she had been certain that his downfall was close at hand. But nothing had happened, nothing of any interest whatsoever. And the waiting had become a burden. It weighed on her mind as soon as she woke up, and would afterwards remain with her throughout the day.

Besides this, she would feel a sense of loss which was hard to locate; and this feeling had been with her ever since she returned from visiting her cousin in Fort William. The day she had walked onto the ferry and felt the solid ground slip away from under her feet, she had been more frightened than at any other time in her life. Across the water, while she held tightly to the ferry rail, she had seen, approaching slowly through the mist, other hills like those she had left behind, and other great boats, similar to those she had seen in the Sound, pass close at hand. But from the minute that she stepped down from the ferry's decks onto dry land, she had walked into a nightmare. The din of the cars and great lorries roaring night and day through the town, the innumerable people running through the streets, the sick, frightened eyes of her cousin, had pinned her dumbly to the ground and prevented her from thinking of anything then but a place where she might hide. Mercifully her cousin had died within the week, and Morag had found her way home again, slowly and with infinite difficulty until she stood at last dumbfounded on Kintillo pier.

Since then she had lost something irretrievable, though what it was and even how she had lost it, she no longer knew. But now, while she went about her work there was a slump to her shoulders and the spring had gone out of her walk, so that she resembled more than ever an old horse put out to grass, which senses in the wind the knacker's yard.

That morning, however, things were vastly

different. She was out of bed with a sharp agility. She neither looked back with regret at the bed she was leaving nor paused while she dressed, to glance at the weather from her bedroom window.

In other ways which were also negative, Morag's later behaviour was equally astonishing. While she served the priest his breakfast she betrayed no emotion whatsoever. She remained quite calm and under control. If her colour was a little heightened, it was due to a certain plan which she had now formed carefully in her mind. When her work in the rectory was done, the beds made and the washing up scrupulously dried and put away, Morag took her army coat from a hook by the kitchen door and went out into the raw cold air of the autumn morning.

The village shop was crowded. Since no one turned to greet her nor paid her the slightest attention, Miss Morag smiled suddenly, a wide triumphant smile, and sat down in a chair by the counter to wait. When she thought of the priest again a joy so wild and terrible flooded through her body that for a moment she felt giddy. She shut her eyes and placed one hand on the counter top to support herself.

When she opened her eyes again the shop was empty, and Jean Macpherson had closed the post office grill.

'If'n you're planning on settling here for the morning,' she said, 'I have work to do and you will be very much in the way.'

'Just a minute,' said Morag getting up from the chair. 'Just a wee minute,' she said again in a wheedling voice. It was all she could do to keep herself from laughing aloud.

The postmistress ignored her. She had two heavy bags of mail beside her on the floor. While she was cutting the string from one of these she said over her shoulder, 'You should know better. Nobody comes in here while I'm sorting the mail. The shop is shut. Shut,' she repeated. She slammed a thick pile of letters down on the counter top behind the grill.

Another wave of laughter surged up in Miss Morag's throat so that when she opened her mouth to speak she began to giggle uncontrollably. Presently she felt weak and sat down again on the chair to rest. 'I have seen them together,' she said calmly, 'the priest and Meriel Finlay.' She watched Jeanie's face. There was nothing there to indicate that she had heard. There was no check in the speed at which she worked. She was sorting letters into piles and around each pile she fixed a rubber band. 'I've seen them,' Miss Morag repeated, 'as clear as day, hugging and kissing together, down by the wooden bridge across the river.'

Without warning Jeanie Macpherson pushed open the grill between them and leant forward. Her face was barely a few inches away from her. 'People say your mother died of syphilis,' she said, separating each word clearly from the next. 'They say that's the reason you're a loonie. I say things are different. I say some are born unfortunate but others are just born wicked. I say you are crazy, eaten up with envy and you always were. Since you were a child, it's those with two eyes the same, normal faces and normal ways, that drove you mad. Now I've seen what's been going on, don't you worry. When Father James came to this parish — and him such a handsome man with fine blue eyes — you couldn't wait, you wicked old bitch, till you had him driven out again.'

Throughout this speech and even when the postmistress had finished, Miss Morag stood by the counter, blinking, as though she had taken in nothing. She shut one eye slowly and then she opened it again and shut the other. 'Now get out!' said Jeanie furiously. She shut the grill again with a snap. 'Now get out of here!'

Miss Morag shook her head. Forgetting her shopping bag and even the food she had come to buy, she turned slowly round and went towards the door. The post office doors were double and one of these was on the latch. In the narrow opening she caught one hip squarely against it and gave a small whimper of pain.

When she was some way down the street, Jeanie Macpherson came out of the village shop and tossed her shopping bag into the middle of the road. Miss Morag turned her back on it and gazed down towards the beach. The tide was going out and the beach was empty. She walked on for about a hundred yards and stopped by the wall to rest. It confused her when people spoke to her too fast. Like a child, she picked out certain words, and turning these over in her mind, she forgot the rest entirely. One single insult however had struck her so forcibly that it was like a blow in the stomach. She sucked in her breath and leant back against the wall. Jeanie Macpherson and the priest had the same blue eyes and they were not merely blue, but of a deep unfaded blue without a flaw. It was this sense of loss, before quite inexpressible, that had haunted her ever since the day when she had first seen her reflection in a mirror.

She stayed by the wall for some time. She noticed nothing around her beyond the one thin branch of an elder bush that the wind shook violently in front of her. And when at last she straightened up and began to walk slowly along the road, she glanced back once at this elder bush as though it were now forever connected in her mind with the blue eyes of the priest.

★ ★ ★

When Morag had gone, the postmistress had some minutes of peace to herself. But instead of continuing with her work, she stood motionless with her hands curled loosely on the counter top and her head bowed. Presently a tear fell on to the counter, and when she had wiped it away, another fell in its place.

The doctor startled her. He came out of the sitting room so quietly that she noticed nothing until he spoke. 'What is it?' he asked. 'What is it, Jeanie?' The postmistress began to work again, more busily than before. There was an obstinate set to her face and small traces of her former anger could be seen in the way she slammed the mail down on the counter and stamped it. 'What is it, Jeanie?' the doctor repeated.

He was comparatively sober; and his words had a sudden authority. After a pause she answered him. 'It was just Morag,' she said, in a voice he could scarcely hear, 'with some wild notion or other that she had in her head.'

' . . . concerning the priest?' Magnus asked thoughtfully.

Jeanie ignored him. 'I cannot abide the woman,' she continued, 'her maundering ways, the mischief that's in her, the loonie voice . . . '

Magnus was silent for a moment. Throughout the last two hours he had been sitting in the parlour next door. He spent an increasing amount of time there, lulled by the warmth of the paraffin stove and the sounds of the shop next door. That morning he had heard through the door, brief snatches of a row between the two women, and now there was a certain hunger in him to hear the rest of it. 'What notion was this?' he asked. 'What story?'

Jeanie shook her head. The mail was sorted at last. There was nothing for her to do — there were no customers to serve and nothing on the counter that needed rearranging. She turned her gaze to the window and stared out across the bay. A low mist had come down over the valley. The landscape was flat and dreary and the trees above the shore stood out, a dull grey against the hill behind.

Magnus was now considering the best way to go on. The highlander is secretive. His loyalties, by reason of his isolated, life, are deep and sometimes inexplicable. Thus, for some reason, Jeanie Macpherson defended the priest, although from whom or from what he could not discover. It did not occur to him that the postmistress feared the effects of his tongue in much the same way that she feared Miss Morag.

He pulled up a chair. It was the same chair on which Morag had sat, a while before, and he leaned his elbows on the counter. When he was sober the doctor had both charm and persuasion. He used these two weapons with gentle cunning on the girl in front of him. 'Listen to me now,' he said softly. 'How long have I known you, Jeanie? How many years is it you have been a solace to me in my loneliness and affliction?'

In spite of herself, the postmistress smiled. 'About ten years I should say,' she replied.

'Ten years, is it?' he seemed surprised at this. 'Ten years . . . That's a grand length of time now. And in that time,' he went on, 'I have never seen you cry. Not under the worst conditions. Not once. And bearing in mind the husband you have, the children and so forth . . . ' he added briskly. 'But this story of the priest — and it does concern him, doesn't it? — now why should it make you cry?'

'Ah, it was nothing, Doctor,' she answered placidly. 'Nothing at all when I think of it.'

Magnus studied her in the same shrewd way that he might have studied the vagaries of a former patient. There were many kinds of lying — half truths, distortions — and he had heard most of them. This last, however, took the biscuit. It certainly took some beating in its simplicity. 'Amongst friends,' he went on patiently, 'there is such as thing as the courtesy of the truth. A politeness, wouldn't you say, that is somehow due between them.'

'Well now,' she answered in the same placid voice, 'the truth is many things, Doctor.' She went over to the window and leant against the sill. 'If the truth was just the one thing, just what you saw now, then we would all be beggars wouldn't we?'

At this moment a little bell rang above the shop door, and Mrs Garvie, a widow from down the street, came in for her morning groceries. She greeted the doctor warmly and started at once to give him the details of her ailments, chilblains and so forth that she had just then remembered. And afterwards when she spoke to Jeanie, her list of groceries was of the same order, an ounce of this, a quarter of that, a fewpenceworth of the other.

With some effort the doctor prevented

233

himself from groaning aloud. He leant heavily on the counter top and began to bite his nails. Mrs Garvie was there for several minutes and when she had gone the silence resumed. But it was now of a different order. There was a certain tension in it for Jeanie had made up her mind to something. She now gave the doctor a look which was swift, subtle and charged with inferences. 'Since you'll hear it from other sources,' she began, 'I'll tell you the story myself. For all,' she added, 'it's not worth repeating.'

Magnus let out his breath in a long slow sigh. He said nothing.

'Aye, it's about the priest,' she said quietly. 'Morag has been spying on him for a time past now. She has it fixed in her head that he's carrying on with some affair.'

'With what affair?' he asked in a whisper. 'With whom?' But he knew quite well who it was before she answered. An ice-cold sickness filled him. For an instant too, he could not breathe. There was a retching sound in his throat and the postmistress leant forward and gazed at him in alarm.

'Are you all right?' she asked.

Magnus straightened himself on the counter. 'Well go on,' he said impatiently, 'go on, go on, finish it for God's sake.'

'That's all there is to it. A storm in a tea

cup. Fancies that she has in her maggotty head. Maybe some trick of the light, the trees moving there down by the bridge.' But she had said too much and was now ashamed of herself. 'The priest is a good and honest man,' she said quickly, 'no matter what he does now.'

Fortunately the doctor was no longer listening. He sat slumped against the counter. After this sudden shock he felt weary and cold. Later he would feel a hatred for the priest which would astound him. But now he stared in a mild, almost bovine way at the postmistress. When he got up from the chair his movements were disconnected as though he had suffered in the last few minutes some form of stroke.

By the counter Jeanie called after him softly. 'If'n there's truth in such a story,' she said, 'it won't all of it be found . . . and besides there are none of us here who will want to know it.'

Before leaving Magnus turned to say good-bye. Against the dark wall behind her and the rows of boxes on the jumbled shelves, her face appeared white and dim. She looked about as real to him as a small wax doll propped up on the counter top.

In the same state of unreality, he wandered home along the road. He had forgotten his car in the village street and it remained there for the night. All forewarnings, premonitions, and such were of no use to him. In a brief span of time he had followed this simple story through to a certain ending. He could see that one day the priest and Meriel Finlay would leave together. They might marry perhaps. But this did not concern him. In any event he would remain alone. As he walked down the road, the puddles in the ruts shone faintly in the sky's reflection. Magnus noticed these and other things in the same way that a sick man, returning slowly to consciousness, would fix his eyes on totally meaningless objects.

From time to time a sudden dizziness came back to him and he staggered slightly on the muddy surface of the road. To the passers-by, when their greetings went unanswered, he resembled the drunken parody of himself that they had often seen going home when the pubs had closed.

Alone on the road, when he had passed the last house between the villages, Magnus sat down on the damp verge by the edge of the road, and began to weep. 'Ah Meriel,' he said over and over again. 'Ah my little Meriel.'

The words brought him a strange comfort. Indeed the very sounds of his grief began to drown the sense of it so that presently he blew his nose loudly and rose to his feet. The hill was steep and Magnus cursed bitterly from time to time as he struggled up the muddy path. The gradient seemed sharper, somehow, and there were boulders in his way that had not been there before. Half way up the slope he stopped for a while to rest. Out in the bay, between the clouds, the sun came down in narrow strips across the water and beyond, towards the sound, patches of the same light flickered on the open sea. It was a view which Meriel had loved. She used to sit by herself sometimes, on the bench outside, watching the sun go down. 'Ah, Magnus,' she had said to him once, 'if I had this view when I was old . . . ' The doctor thought of her now in the past tense, and a dissipated sweetness, for an instant, crossed his face.

'For I have loved her,' he crooned to himself, 'throughout the long days — and most of them alone.'

Later, when he was seated at last in a chair by the empty grate, he amended this statement to himself aloud. 'Not loved her,' he said simply, 'but lusted after her.' Presently he fell asleep in the chair with his head resting on the paraffin stove beside him.

The doctor awoke with a start. There was a knocking at the door. While he searched for his false teeth and fitted them into his mouth the knocking began again. 'I'm coming,' he said loudly.

It took him some time to reach the door; the room was now completely dark and because he had slept very deeply, the furniture seemed to be in unfamiliar places. The laird's factor, Jefferson, stood outside the door with his wife, and Magnus looked at them both with a blank unfocused stare.

'Ah,' said the factor, 'we thought perhaps you'd forgotten . . . '

'You asked us to drinks, now, remember?' Mrs Jefferson said gaily.

'Ah yes,' he said, 'I remember.' He led the way though the cottage door. 'I apologise for the disorder in here, Mrs Jefferson. If you will be so kind as to help me light a few candles round the place, we can all sit down and be comfortable.'

It was biting cold and the candles flickered in every draught that came through the gaps in the door frame. The factor sat totally silent on the edge of a chair and gazed at the floor in front of him as though the entire state of the room and every piece of furniture in it alarmed and disgusted him. Mrs Jefferson also leant forward in her chair and shouted at the doctor, who, because of his age, she imagined to be deaf. Magnus began to mix a little whisky with the sherry he was drinking, and when he could bear Mrs Jefferson's conversation no longer, he removed his false teeth again and wrapped them in a dirty handkerchief which he put into his pocket.

When the Jeffersons had left, he stumbled back in the flickering light towards his rocking chair, where he sat for a time biting his nails. Presently he began to drink again, and briefly, before he was totally drunk, Magnus imagined that Meriel Finlay was somewhere in the cottage and that in a little while she would come into the room with a paraffin lamp and lead him upstairs to bed.

In spite of his drunkenness, for several hours that night he was unable to sleep. He lay on his bed, fully dressed, and with his eyes wide open like a corpse. His head was spinning and his throat was dry. From time to time certain snatches of the past day came back to him; between them the gaps in his memory were total. These gaps were like stones, thrown high into the air, which never hit the solid ground.

19

In small places news travels so fast that at times it seems less to be carried by word of mouth than by the wind. By noon, the Laird's housekeeper had heard in full the story of the village priest and Meriel Finlay. This story she kept to herself, however, for it did not concern her. She had the lunch to prepare and a pie to get ready for the evening meal. But occasionally she would stand by the window, with her work in her hands, a piece of dough she was kneading, or a vegetable half peeled and she would gaze with a puzzled frown into the kitchen yard.

When Meriel came into the room, she did not look up. She was making a steak and kidney pie. Her hands and the front of her apron were covered in flour. 'What's that?' Meriel asked. She watched Mrs Mackinnon roll out the pastry on a marble slab. 'I hope it's steak and kidney — I have a passion for it.'

The housekeeper pursed her lips. 'It is,' she said after a while.

Meriel sat down on a corner of the table. Without looking at her, Mrs Mackinnon could sense a restless vitality in her. She seemed ready to burst out laughing or to spring up without warning and walk about the room.

'How old were you when you married Jock?' Meriel asked presently.

'Nineteen.'

With one hand Mrs Mackinnon took up the pie dish and with a knife she trimmed around the sides. Loose strips of pastry fell in neat crescents on to the table.

'Were you really nineteen . . . imagine . . . how extraordinary.' Suddenly Meriel began to laugh as if there were something amusing in this or a sly and unexpected joke which had just then come into her head.

'Uh huh, nineteen,' said Mrs Mackinnon.

The pastry, when glazed with an egg, would be a fine honey colour, and the meat inside it a rich dense brown. She sighed and put down the dish.

'Well then,' she said, 'what's on your mind?'

Meriel flushed vividly. She slid down off the table and went to lean against the window sill. 'Well, when you were in love . . . ' she began. But here the words sounded trite to her and she did not go on.

'In love? Well, who could you be in love with?' Mrs Mackinnon said crossly. 'You talk as though it was some kind of disease. I've no time for such nonsense.'

But Meriel was not paying attention. She started to speak several times and then suddenly stopped. 'What would you do . . . ' she began. And then a minute later she said, 'And if someone asked you to go away with them — someone you loved . . . not to marry perhaps but just to leave with them, would you go?'

Mrs Mackinnon straightened up from her work. She arranged the knife, the pastry brush and the mixing bowl in a straight line in front of her. And then she looked across the table at Meriel. Her face was bright with anger. 'I have heard rumours today,' she said steadily, 'that I wouldn't credit. I would have none of them. Such a girl I said, brought up a good Catholic, and coming from the best of families, would not be doing such things. Not with a Catholic priest.'

Meriel did not even flinch. She gave the housekeeper a smile that was vague and sweet. 'But we love each other,' she said simply.

Mrs Mackinnon was now so angry that she picked up the mixing bowl in both hands and slammed it down on the table. 'That's no way to be talking,' she cried, 'about a priest of the Catholic Church. There is love, yes, but that's not love, that's sinning. Sinning against your own family and sinning against the Church. I wish,' she added, 'that the Lord might hear you.'

Meriel remained unmoved. Indeed for the time being, she seemed to enclose herself in some place where Mrs Mackinnon and the present reality did not exist. There was a look of obstinate happiness in her face which made the housekeeper fling up her hands in despair. 'I see it's of no use talking to you,' she said. 'I've just been wasting my time and breath. I'm late with the lunch too. If you don't mind I'll get on with it.'

Her anger was spent. She felt drained of the necessary energy to go on with the day ahead of her. She picked up the dirty dishes listlessly and took them to the sink. While she was washing them she looked out of the window again. The first trees around the house were changing colour. A few dead leaves, stirred up by the wind, scattered outwards across the yard. 'God help us,' she said to no one in particular. When she turned round, the room was empty. Meriel had gone. She sat down in a chair and closed her eyes.

'The truth is,' she said later to her husband, 'the truth is, I knew what was going on from a long way back.' And after a while she came to believe it, although the truth was entirely different. The truth was that she had been blind and foolish. When all the events of the past few weeks were added together, Mrs Mackinnon could clearly see what had been going on — so clearly that it now astonished her.

When Nealie the maid came in to the room she got up from the chair. 'I'm going out,' she said. Nealie seemed startled. 'Everything's ready,' she went on quickly, 'the vegetables in the slow oven and the chops in the one above. Take care with the gravy dish,' she added as an afterthought, 'I've just noticed there's a crack in it.'

'When'll you be back?' Nealie asked.

'When I'm ready,' she answered sharply, 'good and ready.'

She took her coat from the back hall peg and walked out into the fresh air. For some time she walked without taking her eyes from the road. She couldn't think what to do now. A while ago there had been nothing on her mind but the cooking, and now this trouble rose up in front of her like a mountain and beyond it, on the other side, she could make out nothing at all. What if they eloped, the two of them? What if the child was already pregnant? What then? And the priest? What of the priest? She shook her head. To these questions and to others which she later asked herself she did not have the answers.

There was one man, however, in whom she had abiding faith, and this was her husband Jock. And here it is necessary briefly, to describe him. For, in the same way that a single pebble, lightly thrown, may start off an avalanche, so it was Jock Mackinnon's advice which set in train the tragedy that followed.

Jock Alistair Mackinnon was a man of great physical strength. He was tall, his shoulders were broad, and his hair was bright red and tightly curled. Throughout the peninsula he was admired for his sound judgement and for his honesty. And if there was a certain blindness in these qualities it was noticed by almost no one, and least of all by his wife. Now Mrs Mackinnon, by the time she reached home, had decided on a certain course. She would listen to her husband's advice and together they would treat the matter in its proper light, as a sorry rumour without any implications.

At once, however, the head keeper took a different attitude. He listened attentively while she spoke and afterwards he was silent for a minute. When he spoke again, his wife felt a chill pass through her like a cold draught that had suddenly come in through an open door. The gossip must be stopped. Things would get worse, he assured her, far worse, unless the Laird's son put an end to them. They would have to be nipped in the bud — he repeated this phrase too in a measured way as though the whole core of the matter lay there. Having spoken at length, the head stalker went on with his meal and dismissed these questions entirely from his mind.

Some time later Mrs Mackinnon went back to the big house to cook the evening meal. The day had lightened at last. A weak sunlight filtered through the trees along the road and their shadows fell in thin strips across the ground. And in the fields to either side of her, the autumn grass shook gently in the wind. Mrs Mackinnon took no comfort whatsoever from such things. She sensed a treachery in the weather, a sweet and dangerous warmth. And beyond that mild September evening she could not forget the long winter that stretched ahead.

She waited until the dinner was served and eaten. And then about nine o'clock she sent Nealie upstairs to turn down the beds, and went herself through the baize door and into the outer hall. Outside the study door she waited for a moment. No sound came from the room. She patted her hair and straightened out the folds of her apron. Then she knocked on the door and went in.

Charles Finlay was alone. Meriel was not about and the old man had been taken back to his room directly after dinner. Mrs Mackinnon closed the door behind her and stood waiting with her hands folded until her employer looked up. 'What can I do for you?' Finlay asked her. He was reading a loose sheaf of papers, in a chair by the fire. These papers concerned the accounts of the syndicate shoot and he disliked any interruption while he was reading them.

'It's about Miss Meriel,' the housekeeper said. But having started she could not go on. The words sounded loose in her throat. The room too, which had been familiar to her all her life, now seemed oddly arranged. Certain pieces of furniture looked out of place and others which she normally took for granted now stuck out strangely.

'Well? Go on.'

Charles Finlay looked briefly into his housekeeper's face. And he saw there an expression of fear which startled him. He got up from his chair by the fire and went towards his desk. 'Well, what is it?' he said impatiently. He had placed himself behind his desk so that the low evening sun shone full into his housekeeper's face while he himself stood to one side, in the shadows.

'It's this way . . . it's like this, sir.' Mrs

Mackinnon now stared at the floor and twisted the corner of her apron about in one hand. 'It seems,' she went on, 'that Miss Meriel is having a love affair with the priest.'

To her astonishment he bent forward for a minute and scribbled something on a sheet of paper beside him on the desk. He put the pen back in the inkstand and shut the lid with a snap. 'What rubbish is this?' he asked her finally. 'What nonsense are you repeating?'

'I don't think it's nonsense, Sir,' she said bravely. 'I think it's the truth, so help me. She was seen last night in the woods with Father James.'

'By whom?'

'By Morag, the housekeeper.'

Finlay gave a loud snort of laughter. 'Hah, then you see. And if that is the only source of your information . . . '

Mrs Mackinnon straightened her shoulders and fixed her employer with a sad, firm look. 'There are others,' she said, 'other sources besides. Nealie for instance. One night when Morag was away, Miss Meriel's bed was not slept in. She was out all night.'

'And then?'

'And then,' she said finally with a sigh, 'I have heard the truth, sir, I have heard it from Miss Meriel herself.'

Charles Finlay came suddenly round the

corner of the desk. He stumbled on a piece of carpet and recovered his balance. In spite of this he moved so fast that she had no time to get out of his way. He took her by the shoulders and began to shake her. 'Shut up,' he whispered. 'Shut up, shut up, shut up!'

His face caught a sudden angle of sunlight. The skin was tightly stretched across the bones, and it had the greenish hue of soft wet clay. A fresh gust of wind began to rattle at the window panes and the same wind, a thin cold draught, came into the room from beneath the mahogany door.

20

Father James had spent a day of acute depression and in the course of the late afternoon he had reached a sudden crisis. That afternoon, while he was drinking tea with one of his parishioners, the priest had done something unaccountable. In the middle of a sentence he had got up from his chair, murmured some brief excuse and walked out of the house. For, suddenly, while sitting alone with this old lady, he had longed to confide in her, to confess everything, and even to imagine in her face, an expression of sympathy and understanding. He had left in such a hurry, that his coat, and a book she had lent him, were still in the old lady's sitting room.

After his evening meal the priest sat alone in his study. The depression had left him finally and in its place he felt a queer lightheadedness. He looked at the contents of the room around him in a mild disinterested way, as though seeing these things for the first time and from a distance.

On his desk and among the folds of his wallet were the details of his transfer to another diocese. In less than two weeks' time, he was leaving Kintillo for a large industrial parish in the north of England. It was an area he had never been to and had scarcely even glanced at on a map. And in his present mood, these facts were about as vital to him as a string of beans. They were merely words to him, and they were words without a single image to support them. Something else disturbed him, a deep irrational longing which the priest no longer resisted: he intended that night, before renouncing her entirely, to see Meriel Finlay again.

He knew exactly how it would be. He knew the house, and also where Meriel slept, for he had seen her once walking along the landing to her room. But to the details of his plan, his walk down the drive at night, and his methods of breaking in, Father James paid almost no attention. He saw instead the inside of the house and the darkened hallway, its upper landings lit by the thin beams of a waning moon. Keeping to the deepest shadows, he would walk noiselessly up the wide staircase and along the moonlit landing to her room. Opening the door slowly and very gradually, he would slip at last inside her room. And here his fantasies sharpened and became more explicit. He could see, in spite of the semi-darkness, the position of the furniture in the room, the varying shades of the night, the same moon, from a gap between the curtains, thrown in a strip of light across the floor. Finally he saw Meriel asleep. In her face there would be a look of warmth and of animal comfort, so totally oblivious, that if he leant across the pillow to kiss her, she would neither stir nor feel his presence.

He sat in the twilight and waited for the darkness. Sitting by the window, it seemed necessary to watch for each separate fleck of the night to appear. And still he could see the long line of the bay and each point and bay beyond, going south to Kyle. And when he looked around the study, although colour had been drawn from the room and the shadows had deepened and merged together, he could still see well enough to pick out each crack in the walls, and each mark of damp on the ceiling. His back ached from sitting in the same position; the whole of his body felt numb, as though the blood was no longer circulating and had centred at last in a dense mass around his heart.

Morag had gone to bed some time ago. Out of boredom he had counted every step of the stairs as she went up to bed. There were fourteen of them and on each tread her weight had given out a different creaking note. Later he listened to the sound of her movements in the passage upstairs. They seemed erratic, one footfall heavier than another, and each of her journeys to and from the bathroom were accompanied by a low sibilant muttering.

Slowly the rectory settled into a torpid silence. One noise after another, the vibration of the upstairs cistern, the water circulating in the pipes, had gradually faded. And now after a day of tension the priest felt drowsy and relaxed. In spite of his cramped position in the upright chair, his eyelids closed and his head fell sideways against the window-sill. While he slept he began to dream.

In the last of these dreams before waking, he was lying in his bed at home and through the open window of his room, the branches of a great hibiscus were growing in thick profusion. The leaves of the tree were a sickly green and its flowers pressed in big scarlet clusters around the window frames. The heat in the room was damp and oppressive and the silence total.

When he awoke, it was daylight. At first he looked around him in disbelief. In the wake of this vivid and meaningless dream the room seemed quite without substance. The clothes he was wearing also seemed strange — a thick sweater and dark grey trousers. He could no longer remember changing into them nor could he remember for some minutes why he was sitting there.

Suddenly and with a sense of shock, he put a hand in one pocket. He felt there the edges of a letter. It was the letter which he had written to Meriel Finlay. And then too he remembered the evening before, and the wild notion he had had of slipping this letter under her pillow while she slept. But the morning had come and he had done nothing. With every minute that passed the room was becoming lighter. Already the shadows had faded and the colours around him were stronger and more distinct.

For a moment Father James gave in to an extraordinary panic. His face flushed and his hands began to tremble. He had left things too late to set out now in the daylight, for he was certain to be seen going into the house. And yet it was unthinkable to leave without seeing her. He felt this indecision so acutely that, without realizing what he was doing, he began to walk rapidly up and down the room — now deciding he would go immediately, now convinced that he could not do it.

Finally he took the letter and went towards the fireplace. He took a box of matches from the mantlepiece and firmly struck a light. He was about to hold this light to a corner of the letter when he looked up quickly as though something had disturbed him. He blew out the match and put the letter back in his pocket. For a minute in his mind he had seen Meriel. She ran headlong through the open fields towards him, as though reaching the scene of some disaster. And in her face he could see a look of rootless terror.

He sat down and covered his face with his hands. 'That's nonsense,' he said aloud. 'That's all nonsense.' Nevertheless, he now wanted to see her more than ever. He wanted to assure himself that Meriel still lay as he had imagined her, in a deep untroubled sleep. He was afraid for her in some vague way he could not describe. And now, sitting in the silent room, it seemed to the priest that his fears were not caused by his own heightened nervousness, but by certain forces outside himself, by some insidious warning in the atmosphere which he could not explain. At the same time a strange apathy came over him so that he went on sitting, without moving, in the chair.

When he looked up at last and went to the window, the daylight had finally come. The peaks of the Cuillins were clear across the water. To the north of them, to the east and to the south, other mountains, colourless in the early sun, rose steeply from the sea.

'I should go now,' he thought. 'I should really go.' But he stayed a little longer looking out of the window.

★ ★ ★

It was half past four in the morning when Meriel awoke. She woke up quite suddenly as though someone had called her name. And afterwards she lay without moving in the bed, for it seemed to her that the silence was incomplete and that presently this voice, on the same high note, would call out to her again. But the sound was not repeated. There was nothing outside her window but the sound of the first birds among the trees around the house. First one close by among the branches of a great magnolia and then others further away among the fringes of the woods. While she listened to them she smiled. It seemed to her that in the wake of each song a tree would bloom and take shape again after the night.

Presently she put on her slippers and dressing gown and went to the window. The sky was a light, clear grey and below it the line of Raasay was flat against the sea. On such mornings the light would draw downwards from the peaks across the coast of Skye; the sea from grey would turn to a frail

256

pure blue and the birds would spread their full wing span when the sun had risen and begin their hunt for food. But there were other mornings, cold and dense, when the light lifted slowly like a mist, from the ground upwards. Certain shapes appeared gradually and in a certain order: the line of trees along the wall of the park, the creeks and hollows of the bay, and then finally the islands in the Inner Sound. On those mornings the sea was calm and sullen, confined to a space without horizons. But now the dawn was cloudless and in less than an hour the sun would light up the sound and the Inner Hebrides beyond it.

Her window faced south. The rectory was out of sight, on the side of the hill. And yet her whole attention was drawn towards it as though she were there in the room watching the priest while he slept. When she thought of him she was filled with an extraordinary happiness. This happiness made her restless so that it was no longer possible to stay dreaming by the window nor to go back again to her bed. Without having the slightest idea where she would go, she began to dress hurriedly and a few minutes later with her shoes in one hand went down the stairs into the dark hall. By the door she slipped on her shoes and a coat from the peg and went out.

The hinges of the front door creaked when she shut it behind her, and she stood for a moment listening on the steps outside. The gun dogs lived in the stables. At the faintest sound they would bark and fling themselves at the tack room door. Her father, too, slept lightly. He would sometimes wake up when she went out in the early morning and she would see his face at the bedroom window as she was going across the park.

She kept to the grass verges along the edge of the house and walked on the drive where the gravel was thin and worn into the ruts. From time to time she looked back at her father's window which faced west over the sound and to the north across the side woods and the open valley. Because of the early hour and the emptiness of the park around her she felt a certain guilty pleasure as if she were doing something expressly forbidden.

In the darkness of the woods a pheasant rose from the bushes close to the path and its disconnected cry seemed to scatter out across the whole of the valley. The noise startled her and she walked on more cautiously until she came to the bridge across the river. From the rickety wooden bridge the path ran through the trees into the flat marsh fields of the valley bottom.

Meriel took the road to Loch Doonican. From the heights of the small peat loch she would see the coast of Skye and the line of the mainland going south to Kyle. She would sit by the empty shooting lodge along the shore and raise her face to the first warmth of the sun when it came up across the rim of Torridon. She walked so lightly on the ground that she seemed to float above it and each step carried her forward with a strange weightlessness.

When she was still a child the summer had seemed like this: the mornings grey, the sunsets violent and queerly coloured, and the days themselves cloudless and without wind. In those summers they had spent all day, she and Anne, on the empty beaches. They would take picnics down to the edge of the shore and they would fool around there until it was warm enough to bathe. And with the same uncomplicated joy she felt now, Meriel would run out across the sand too fast to stop herself from wading clear into the sea. The fierce cold of the water would shock her and at the same time she would burst out laughing as the spray shot up around her in the sun. But now she despised this former happiness and even thought of it with pity. For she had been easily satisfied. In the course of a single warm day she had forgotten the weeks of rain which had preceded it.

Now her emotions were of another calibre. They were deeper and more intense. They had roots to them, or a single solid base: her mind and heart were totally concerned with the priest and her feelings were directed towards him in the same natural way that a flower in the shadows of a room would turn towards the light.

The fenced-in fields of the valley were now below her and the brown wastes of the moors came down to the edges of the road. The moors were pitted with bogs and deep hollows which were as neat and as round as wells. From these hollows the marsh birds rose up into the morning sun. Meriel began to sing to herself aloud. Although the song was sad, she sung it gaily and in a high lilting voice:

'Early one morning, just as the sun was rising

I saw a maiden singing in the valley below.

Oh don't deceive me,

Oh never leave me.

How could you use a poor maiden so.'

There was only one verse to it — a verse of five lines — and she sang it without thinking, over and over again. There were no trees around the peat loch Doonican, nothing to retain the sound. Her voice seemed to stop a few feet from her and the silence of the empty moors remained unbroken.

★ ★ ★

Charles Finlay had heard his daughter go out for he had been awake throughout the long pale night. He heard the latch of her bedroom door open and gently close again. He had heard the stair-treads creak and the hinges of the great front door hiss and swing shut behind her. He listened to these things without surprise, for he told himself that everything was now clear to him — not only what had previously taken place but the exact order of the events which would follow. He knew Meriel was walking up the road towards the rectory, and that in a few minutes the priest would appear in the doorway and let her into the house. At the thought of the priest, an odd smile crossed his face, and in the dimness of the room this smile resembled the fixed grin on the face of a stiffened corpse.

Presently he got up and started to dress. He dressed without hurrying and in his normal methodical fashion. Since the early morning was certain to be damp and cold, Finlay took from his cupboard a pair of plus-fours and a thick tweed jacket. There was nothing in his mind at all. It was a total blank fixed only on the task in hand, as though one set of actions however trivial, was now as important as another. When he was dressed, he took his stiletto knife from a table and into the breast pocket of his jacket he tucked a loosely folded handkerchief. Finally he stood for a minute looking out of the window. Like someone in a dream, he saw nothing. His vision was turned inwards and his face was calm and even cold.

Before leaving, his eyes wandered slowly round the room as though there was something he had forgotten which he would shortly remember. In his chest of drawers there was a box of cartridges. He took two of these from the box and slipped them into his left hand pocket. From a corner of the room, by the cupboard, he took his shotgun and held it lightly in the crook of his arm. After a moment's thought, however, he opened the chambers and lifted it to the light. Both barrels were clean and well oiled. Finlay sighed and rearranged the gun on his arm. Once again he looked around the room before going out and shutting the door quietly behind him.

Outside the sun had fully risen. The dew was heavy on the ground and the whole park glistened in the fresh morning light. But

Finlay noticed nothing for his reactions were hardened and blunted by shock. In this state of shock, which had been with him throughout the night, he again told himself that he understood everything and that what he had to do was both right and inevitable. He carried his gun easily and naturally, and his eyes were fixed on the drive in front of him as he walked along.

A keen wind was coming in from the west and the wash of a storm at sea rolled in across the wide mouth of the bay. The sound of the sea was as natural to him as the sound of his own breathing and he neither looked up nor lessened his speed against the force of the rising wind. Something else, scarcely audible, attracted him — the sound of footsteps coming down the rectory hill.

When he looked up and saw the priest, he noticed first the clothes he was wearing, a thick Arran sweater and a pair of grey corduroy trousers. His hair was ruffled by the wind, and shone brightly in the early sun. In his right hand he was holding a white envelope and this too caught the light. Finlay took in these details in the same way that a man might notice the moss or the patterns in the brickwork of a well down which he was falling.

In the time it took for the priest to look up

at him, Charles Finlay had loaded the gun and raised it to his shoulder. At a distance of thirty yards he aimed for the centre of his forehead and fired two shots. Father James fell forward into the road without a sound. A few pebbles scattered loose around his body and ran free for a little way among the ruts of the road.

Finlay ejected the cartridges from the gun and stood for an instant motionless in the road. He neither looked up at the point where the priest had fallen, nor did he think of him. Something perplexed him. In the few seconds before firing, a sound had disturbed him: in the lull of the wind he had heard a voice singing across the valley fields. But now, though he listened, the singing had stopped.

THE END